CHAPTER 1

Fear strangled my heart as my magic swirled around me like a dark tornado. Maybe I was the blood witch, and no amount of sugarcoating would change my destiny. I could feel the reality of my surroundings shift as if I were tearing the fabric of time and space. Long tendrils of shadow wrapped around me like inky fingers as the training facility began to fade away.

I tried to stop what was happening, to halt the geyser of power erupting from my core, but the boundaries of the room continued to blur as my magic responded to some ancient call within. It was a primal power intent on my survival, and the cut at my throat had unleashed something I couldn't control.

The air crackled with energy as my hands fisted at my sides and I prayed I didn't destroy everything and everyone around me. Amidst the tsunami of chaos, I heard Cass call out.

"Raven, you need to control it. I can't see you."

Cass confirmed my fears. I was creating a shroud. Probably the same magic the traitorous witch was using to pop in and wreak havoc before disappearing without a trace. My body was still in the room, but an experienced witch could hide in the shadows and bend light around themselves, so they were invisible to the naked eye.

"I can't stop it," I yelled. My power surged again, and I closed my eyes tightly to attempt to rein it in. The rookie mistake of Kirnen's blade had set off a rush of power that threatened to overwhelm me. There were legends of powerful witches who had destroyed themselves because they possessed too much power and didn't learn to control it. There hadn't been a witch like that for hundreds of years, but here I was, about to obliterate myself.

The shroud was like a one-way mirror. While Cass could not see me, she and Kirnen were fully visible. The rookie death dealer stumbled to his feet with an expression of shock and trepidation. While he couldn't see me, he could sense the power pulsating in the room as Cass stared at me with determination. I knew that look. She would sacrifice herself to save me, but she had no idea what to do.

Part of me was surprised Rene hadn't busted down the door and demanded me to stop. I tried to draw on my training as a young witch and anchor my power, but I had possessed so little when I was alive those techniques did nothing to lessen the flow and the shadows consumed me further, as if my very essence were slipping away.

Cass reached for the bolas she had dropped on the ground when my magic had blasted outward. I hadn't seen it burst from her hand, but she had likely been more concerned about me and Kirnen.

She hoisted the weighted cord and began to spin it in the air. Her eyes flicked from one side of the shadows to the other and I knew she was guessing at my location within it. The stones at the end spun so quickly I could no longer track them and when she released them, it was like a propeller in the air. This time they were aimed low, and I yelled when they impacted my knees.

FORTY DEATHS TILL US PART

A MAGICAL MIDLIFE DEATH NOVEL

TIA DIDMON

Forty Deaths till us Part

I love hearing from my readers so please contact me at:
https://tiadidmon.com

Other books in this Series
Forever Forty
Forty Proof and Dead
Forty Shades of Dead
Forty Days and One Vampire Night
Forty Reasons to Die
Forty Deaths till us Part
Forty is the New Dead

More books are coming in this series. Check out https://tiadidmon.com/book-list/ for the complete list.

The force sent me forward, but the thick cord held my legs fastened together and I crashed to the floor with a loud thump. The shadows began to rise, attempting to feed off my power as the room trembled, but the darkness began to fade and Cassara's eyes focused on me, alerting me I was within her line of sight. My shoulders shook as the last traces of power faded like a receding tide.

I moved to a sitting position as Rene stormed through the door. His eyes went between Cass and me and he looked angry, but unsure. It probably looked like Cass had thrown the bolas to test me.

"What is going on? I felt a disturbance," he asked.

I began to unwrap the bolas around my legs as Cass stood.

"We had a little incident. I am not sure if it is because I used the bolas on her the first time or if Kirnen accidentally cutting her, had an adverse effect, but her power... exploded."

Rene knelt down beside me as I pulled the bolas from my body and placed it on the floor. "It wasn't the weapon. When Kirnen cut me... something happened. My power expanded. Or I accessed something dormant. It is hard to explain, but I didn't have any control over it. I'm just glad Cass was here to use the bolas on me."

Rene helped me to my feet. "It's the reason I had one assigned to you. There is nobody to help you with this aspect of your training. Cass will carry the bolas, so if you need assistance, she is there for you. It will not be used to constrain you. Just to diminish your magic if you have an outburst."

I should have known that Rene would consider the safety of those around me. Hell, that bolas had saved my life. "Thank you. I didn't realize how much I needed something like that, but Cass thinks I will be able to overcome its effects, eventually. It isn't like a witch box."

"I am aware of that, but by the time you learn to circumvent

the bolas, you will have learned to control your magic. This is just
an interim safety precaution."

Kirnen and Cass approached us, but I could see the young
death dealer was apprehensive. "May I ask how you can be so
powerful? I was unaware that any witch possessed such skill."

Rene put his hand on the small of my back. "It is because she
is mine. Kirnen you will keep these events private from the clan.
You may only discuss any concerns about this incident with Cass
or the other death dealers."

Kirnen nodded. "Raven, I did not mean to cut you. My blade
slipped when you countered my last attack. I assumed since you
were a fledgling, you would be slower. There is no excuse for my
error."

Guilt was a bitch, and I hated it. He felt this event was his
fault.

"Kirnen, I had no idea this would happen, so there's no way
you could have. Vampires heal from a simple cut. I should never
have blasted you into the weapons wall and for that, I'm sorry. All
I can do is promise that I'll have more control the next time we
spar."

Kirnen looked me over cautiously. It was hard to tell what he
was thinking, and he had every right to be leery of me. Had he
been human, he would be dead right now? "May I return to my
quarters? I didn't rest after returning home. I apologize again for
cutting you." He nodded respectfully to Rene when the overseer
released him by motioning toward the door. And he strode toward
the exit.

The click of the door closing echoed through the massive
room as if we were in a tomb and I put my hand over my eyes to
stay my tears. What the hell was wrong with me? I knew Kirnen
wasn't trying to kill me. Nobody did that in front of Cassara. He
hadn't lied when he apologized. He felt responsible for my

outburst. No wonder the clan didn't trust me. I couldn't even trust myself.

Rene pulled my hand away from my eyes. "Raven, tell me what happened? Cass looks like she has seen a ghost. What kind of magic did you call forth?"

"That's a loaded question. I have seen it before, but I never possessed this magic."

He glanced at Cass. "You have seen it before? You mean you are taught its use in witch school?"

I shook my head. "They didn't teach that kind of magic in school. Nobody had that kind of magic. I had never seen it before the traitor."

Rene's eye flickered. "What?"

Cass wet her lips. "She created the shadow thing that the witch traitor uses to mask her presence. Raven was encased in shadow and hadn't disappeared yet, but she was close."

Rene's eyes narrowed on me. "How does this magic work? What is it called?"

My shoulders sagged. "I wish I knew. The only thing I can compare it with is a form of shroud. The shadows form around me and then the light begins to alter the exterior. The closest thing I can compare it to is a cloaking device. This is the magical version and until that nasty witch used it, I had never seen it before. Now that I have experienced it, I can feel how it works, but I don't know how to turn it off. Once I began feeding the magic, it didn't want to let go."

Rene's eyes narrowed on me. "Your magic is evolving far too rapidly. Do you have any idea why?"

I grunted. "You may as well ask me why I died, or why I survived transition. I'm sorry, but there is no explaining what I am or what I am turning into."

Rene pulled me against him. "Do not worry about it. We will take all the necessary precautions to keep you safe."

I searched his eyes. "How?"

He touched my face gently, brushing his knuckles over my cheek. "We will contact Ursula and get those tests. We will appear to be acceding to her wishes, but they will reveal all your magics so we have a better understanding of your power and how to control it."

While trusting Ursula was about the last thing I wanted, I had grown up with witches and knew how the tests worked. They would give me the information I needed as well as access to the high priestess' knowledge. She wouldn't want a more powerful witch than her roaming around unfettered, and I was beginning to suspect I was exactly that. How I had become this was still a mystery. One I may never solve.

Rene stared at me for some time, and I frowned. "Raven, can I contact her? I would never do so without your permission."

I was about to remind him that he was the overseer, but I smiled ruefully. "Yes. I appreciate you asking me. I will do the tests."

Rene took out his cell phone and pulled up Ursula's contact. She picked up on the first ring. "Ursula, Raven will do the test tonight; make the necessary arrangements." He was quiet for some time. "I will make no further concessions. Either have things ready for us tonight or we will not accede to your wishes." He hung up.

Cass folded her arms. "What did the witch say?"

Rene kept his eyes on me. "She is making all the necessary arrangements. We will go to the coven building at dusk."

I nodded, and my eyes drooped. While my power had seemed endless when it was cascading out of me like a rushing waterfall, my stamina appeared to lack the same enthusiasm. "Okay."

Rene took my hand. "You are tired. Expending your magic drains you quickly. We will retire until dusk."

My eyes met Cassara's. "Thank you for helping me."

She shrugged casually. "It was nothing."

Rene cleared his throat. "It was not nothing. She could have expended all her power had you not acted so quickly. A witch dies if she drains her life force using magic. I do not wish to test that premise with Raven."

Cass held the back of her hand to her mouth. "He is just pissed I got to tie you up before he did."

The laugh escaped my lips before the image of me bound naked made my heart stutter.

Rene sighed. "Please check on Kirnen."

He led me from the training facility and almost every vampire kept their gaze on the floor. I had no idea what havoc my magic had caused in the rest of the mansion, but it was obvious they felt it.

I breathed a sigh of relief when we ascended the stairs, and we were alone in the hallway. Our suite was pristine and comforting as we entered. "I need a shower."

Rene grabbed the hem of my blouse and pulled it up over my head. "That is a good idea."

I put my hand on his wrist when his fingers moved to my pants. "I can undress myself. You don't have to shower with me."

He moved closer to me and didn't relinquish his hold. "But I want to, and you are barely able to stand by yourself. You are exhausted and I would never take advantage of such a situation, so you are quite safe... today."

It was implied that tomorrow was a whole different story, and a shiver of anticipation skated up my spine. I allowed him to remove my clothes before he discarded his and I followed him to the shower.

He turned on the tap and checked that it was warm before guiding me into the large marble shower. The water cascaded down my skin and seemed to wash away my sins as Rene grabbed a vanilla-scented shampoo from the shelf. He lathered it into my hair as I relaxed into him.

There was something decidedly soothing and decadent about someone else washing your hair, and I found I liked it a lot. "I could get used to this."

His lips were at my ear and his words were far louder than the shower of water. "I expect you too."

My heart stuttered, and I froze as he rinsed the shampoo from my hair.

"Relax Raven. It is just a shower."

Yeah, that was easy for him to say. I was completely reliant on him and would be dead if it weren't for Cass and him. I took the towel from him and wrapped it around my body when he passed it to me before following him back to the bedroom.

He dried off and ended by using the towel to get the excess water from his hair. It was hell on a woman with any kind of libido to witness him naked, and I turned away and proceeded to dry myself. If I kept staring at him, I would not be getting any sleep and Rene was right. I needed it.

My body tensed when he touched my shoulder. "Get into bed, Raven."

CHAPTER 2

J woke in the soft embrace of Rene's bed; the night had set, and I could see clouds through the filtered moonlight and the cracked curtains. As I stretched beneath the cool, luxurious sheets, Rene's hand slid over my stomach. I tried to avoid thinking about the events in the training facility and the memories of last night's shower and his gentle touch flooded back, warming me.

The water had cascaded over my skin, in a soothing caress that washed away the pain of my actions. His eyes were on me with a mix of hunger and concern, but he kept the promise that rest was paramount and had simply taken me to bed.

I had marveled at his selflessness, how he hadn't risen from the bed, and remained like a sensual sentry at my side, despite not needing the rest himself. His fingers had traced soothing patterns on my back. As if he were writing a script in an ancient language only he could read. I was aware he was branding me in some way. Making a silent promise that he would guard me until I rose.

When my eyes had closed and sleep had snatched me from the waking world, I had felt cared for in a way I had never known before. The tenderness reminded me of the growing connection between us. I was falling in love with him, and that was scarier than any magic or enemy.

Rene kissed my cheek. "Are you ready to face the high priestess?"

I put my hand over my eyes. "I was literally just thinking this was a wonderful way to wake up. But you just ruined it."

Rene chuckled. "I would much rather remain in bed with you than meet with Ursula."

I slipped my hand around his neck and pulled him closer. My lips touched him gently and as our kiss became more fevered, he growled into my mouth.

"We could play hooky," I whispered eagerly.

"I am unfamiliar with that term," Rene said."

I winked. "It's when you skip class."

"I think we need to keep this appointment. Are you always going to entice me with sex to attempt to get your way?"

My jaw dropped before I snapped it shut. "That depends on if it would work."

He leaned closer, so his lips touched mine. "In many cases, it would."

I swallowed hard. "Good to know."

Rene rolled out of bed with the gracefulness of a cheetah, and I scooched to the side as he entered the closet. It didn't matter which of the hundred suits in there he chose. He would look like he just stepped into a photo shoot.

I slipped from the bed fully naked and entered the closet. Rene had chosen a black suit but was only wearing the pants. He was doing up his shirt as I moved to my side of the closet and began to flick the hangers to the side.

"Are you stalling, Raven?" he asked.

My fingers paused on a dark-blue pantsuit. It wasn't something I would have worn normally, but it was beautiful, and I decided to try it. "I was just allowing you to admire the view."

Rene leaned toward me and kissed my cheek. "Then I appreciate your thoughtfulness." He left the closet with his suit jacket in his hands as I pulled on my undergarments.

I slipped on the tailored pants and marveled at how well they fit me before choosing a cream blouse. I slipped on the matching jacket and accessorized with a tan belt. I had to admit I felt like a million bucks when I left the closet to join Rene and his appreciative gaze alerted me he agreed with my assessment.

Rene was ready, looking like a Greek god, so I dipped into the bathroom and quickly brushed my hair before we exited the suite. There were always glances of apprehension when I descended the stairs to the parlor, but several men glanced at me with obvious interest. While everyone knew I was Rene's fledgling, they were oblivious to our relationship. I couldn't blame them for that either. As amazing as I looked, Rene was otherworldly beautiful.

Cass was waiting for us by the front door, and she opened it to allow us to exit. The limo was in place at the end of the canopy, and we passed the series of lights that accented the shrubs before getting into the back seat.

Rene guided me beneath his arm as we pulled away. "These tests do not hurt the witch in any way, correct?"

I patted his leg. "Not at all. Every magic has a signature of sorts. Provided it is not a brand-new magic and something that a coven member possessed at some time in history, the high priestess can identify it."

"What if you possess a new magic?"

I shrugged. "It's possible, but unlikely. We are talking about every witch that ever lived."

Rene shifted in his seat as the hum of the road attempted to soothe my frayed nerves, but the closer we got to the coven building, the more I fidgeted.

Cass leaned forward in her seat. She was wearing one of her favorite one-piece leather suits, but no jacket and her weapons were distinct and threatening on her belt. "We don't have to do this, Raven. I don't care what Rene or Ursula say."

I smiled. "Thank you, Cass, I appreciate that. I do. But I need to know what is going on with me... magically speaking. I seem to have ridiculous amounts of power, and I don't want to be out of control again. If I don't get myself sorted out, I could hurt someone, and that is not an option. Every witch has to swallow her pride at some point in her life."

Cass leaned back in her seat. "Really? I don't get the impression that Ursula has tasted much in the way of crow."

I chuckled. "True. While it's a bit before my time, I have heard the stories. Ursula began to develop her magic, far younger than most witches do. She was more powerful than any other coven member by the time she was nineteen. So yeah, she doesn't know what it's like to be second best."

Cass crossed her arms. "Until now. Have you considered that she is jealous of you?"

I pursed my lips. "There's no way to know I'm more powerful than her. No one in the coven knows the true extent of her magic, with the exception of Brigid. The high priestess must groom her second and that is Brigid."

Cass glanced at Rene. "Your magic isn't the only thing she is jealous of."

I frowned. "She hates vampires. Regardless of how hot Rene is, she would never be jealous of our... relationship. She can't even be sure I have one with him."

"It's obvious to most people Rene is taken with you, but it isn't his looks she is jealous of."

"His power."

Cass nodded. "Ursula is like every high priestess ever born in that regard."

I contemplated her words as we drove the rest of the way to the coven building. The gravel crunched beneath our tires and my shoulders sagged. Cassara's assessment made me even less enthusiastic about my impending tests.

We entered the coven building to find Ursula and Brigid standing at the head of the table. There were various crystals, potions, and other implements on the polished wood. I recognized many of the items from my testing as a teen, but several were new to me.

The high priestess stood like a figure of ageless wisdom and her eyes held an ancient knowledge, but they gazed at me with a mixture of trepidation and anger. When she beckoned me closer with a curt gesture, I feared Cass was right.

"We will begin the tests. I will start with proprietary powers. This is the same test you took as a young girl."

Rene moved closer to me. "Explain the tests to me."

I touched his arm. "This test will expose telekinesis, protection barriers, glamors, and other similarly common powers."

Cass nodded. "We know you have those. What is the test called?"

"This is the test of bronze. The most common powers belong to this category."

Cass grunted. "Like the witch Olympics. That's just great."

I pursed my lips so I wouldn't laugh. "Yeah, basically. But some bronze-level magics are still very powerful."

She shrugged. "I noticed that when you blasted Kirnen."

Ursula pointed to the circle of salt near the table. "Stand in the circle, Raven."

I moved to the salt circle as instructed and waited for the first test. Ursula flicked her wrist, and a bronze-colored fire ignited the circle. She could make that fire any color, but the high priestess was a traditionalist, and the fire moved toward the middle before winding its way up my legs. It danced over my clothes, but this was a fire of magic and there was no heat and no pain. It swirled around me as if I was its lover and continued to move upward on my body. The hue changed as it hit my chest. Flickers of blue, silver, and pink. There were too many to name, and I stared at the rainbow of color in awe.

Brigid paled and turned to Ursula. "All of them. She has every bronze power."

The flame died away as I considered her words. I didn't even know what all the bronze powers were; a witch only trained on the ones she possessed. "You will tell me what those are, right?"

Ursula nodded. "You will be provided with all the information you need. Let's finish the tests."

I remained in the circle as Ursula took a vial filled with a light-purple liquid. Lavender helped create the beautiful color and scent. I had grown the ingredients for that potion when I'd been alive and owned the flower shop.

Brigid took the potion from Ursula and walked over to hand it to me. Her black robes moved like ribbons in the wind as she passed it to me. "Drink it," she said curtly.

I recognized every element in that potion and my senses came alive. "Lavender, mink oil, moon lace, Grecian salt, and amethyst." While the ingredients were important, it was the spell used on the potion that would reveal my magic. I downed the vial.

The tingling feeling traveled from my throat and spread outward. I flipped my palm up before a vine grew from my palm. "That is my original power." When my opposite hand tingled, I flipped it up and fire erupted on the other.

Brigid hissed. "Fire magic? That should not be."

There was a cloud of smoke in both hands next, and I looked at Ursula when she stepped forward.

"You have two unidentified magics," she said in awe and fear.

I gave Rene a dirty look. "You jinxed me. I told you I was a unicorn."

Rene smiled, but his eyes remained on Ursula and Brigid. He

may have agreed to bring me here, but he didn't trust the elder witches at all. "I assume that was the silver test?"

Ursula pointed to the table. "Yes. This is the gold. Brigid, give her the mirror," she said rudely.

Brigid's eyebrows furrowed, but she grabbed the intricately-carved silver mirror from the table. It was able to reveal a seer, but I had no precursors for such a magic and had never held it.

She brought it to me and held it out to me ceremoniously. "Here. Stare into it and see if it reacts to you."

I took the hand-held mirror that looked like it was from another era and turned the reflective surface toward me. At first there was nothing except my reflection, but slowly the background in the mirror began to blur. While my face stayed the same, I began to see glimpses of an untraveled path. A healer. A teacher. A botanist. The last was the most like me, but the clothing I wore was from some forgotten era. "Are these my past lives?"

Ursula glanced at Brigid with concern. "She should see her future, not her past lives."

Brigid glanced down nervously. "If her magic is stronger than that of the first seer, then she is not bound by its rules."

Ursula's lip twitched. "Impossible. The first seer was the most powerful witch ever born. They were strict with breeding then. There was no human dilution in those days."

My eyes flickered. "Human dilution? Are you flipping kidding me?"

Ursula rolled her eyes. "I didn't make the rules then, Raven. The witches and warlocks were very particular about mixing bloodlines. Marriages were approved and... arranged to ensure powerful progeny."

I grunted. "I bet you wish you could still get away with that bullshit."

Ursula pointed at the mirror. "Brigid, take the mirror and test for outliers."

"What are outliers?" Rene asked.

I pointed to the various objects on the table. "They are magics that are extremely rare. Usually, only one or two witches have ever had them. They are too unusual to be included in the bronze or silver test. As you may have noticed, they consider a true seer to be the highest form of magic. I didn't see my future, so I don't think I possess that power."

Ursula looked relieved by that, but she didn't like the result I had with the mirror either. "Touch the objects on the table, Raven."

I exited the salt circle and began to touch the artifacts sitting there. The black crystal did nothing, but the old cloth produced a dark shadow.

"A shroud," Ursula said with wonder.

A few objects sent a tinge of awareness through me, but no others reacted visibly. I said nothing about these objects, as Ursula looked like she was ready to lash out. Suggesting I may be more powerful was the last thing I wanted.

"That's it," I said as I touched a clear crystal with no effect.

Ursula nodded, but I could practically see the wheels turning in her brain. "The coven needs to monitor Raven's progress. There are two unidentified magics and her reaction to the mirror is disconcerting. She will need training and only myself or Brigid are willing to take her under our wing."

Rene growled. "This was not our agreement. You put it in writing, which means if you attempt to breach it in any way, you are in direct violation of the conclave. Once this test is over, Raven has no further ties to the coven. All future requests go through me."

Ursula pointed at Rene. "You know nothing of magic. You are

so busy trying to bed her that you can't see the danger that she poses. She may even be a threat to you and your rule as overseer."

Rene arched one eyebrow. "That is a risk I am willing to take. Unlike you, I believe she is worth it."

Ursula hissed. "She is a plague." Her magic began to rise, but I sensed the incline and mine sought to protect Rene and Cass.

The protection barrier was invisible, but Ursula felt it form. "How dare you!"

I grunted. "This coming from the witch that tried to kill me. I am done with your tests, and I suggest you don't push me. I've had enough of the coven and its politics."

Ursula's eye flickered with power. "Then you are dead to the coven."

"Well, it's about time."

CHAPTER 3

I flopped into the back of the limo before Rene closed the door behind Cassara. The vehicle pulled away from the building, and I hoped it was the last time I would be forced to visit the coven. How ironic when I had grown up looking for Ursula's approval.

Cass crossed her legs casually and leaned back in her leather seat. "Ursula is a piece of work, but she lets her anger get the best of her and she is already regretting her outburst."

I crossed my arms. "She regrets nothing. She has always taken pride in making those of us with little magic miserable. It's the coven way or the highway, and she was happy to show me the door."

Rene's finger traced my neck lightly. "I am afraid I have to agree with Cassara in this case. She has no control over you now. Until she allowed her anger to lash out, she had a viable claim to you as a witch. This turn of events is better than I could have hoped."

My jaw dropped. "Excuse me?"

Rene pulled me closer to him. "You are solely mine now. Her

outburst was detrimental to her position. She gave up the only rightful claim she had on you. All because you opposed her."

I glanced at Cassara. "You would never give up one of your own for trash-talking you."

Cass laughed. "I would have been kicked from the clan a thousand times over by now if Rene was so easily offended. Had I known Ursula was so vain, I would have verbally attacked her myself. I am going to start a pool at the clan on this one."

Rene gave Cass a withered look. "Surely you have better things to do."

"Not really. Vampires love to gamble, and it is only a matter of time before Ursula contacts you and wishes to mend fences."

I blinked several times. "A pool? Like guess the weight and sex of someone's baby before it's born? You would gamble on Ursula's indiscretion?"

Cass nodded. "With pleasure and the whole clan will love it." She began to text into her phone as I leaned toward Rene.

"She is kidding, right?"

Rene sighed. "I am afraid not. You being ostracized from the coven will be common knowledge soon. And the high priestess will regret her decision on this. It is a viable pool and vampires do like to gamble on more... unique bets."

I wasn't sure that the clan would care what was going on with the coven let alone bet on it, but I was still too mad at Ursula. If I was honest, it was the assumption that she was taking something of value from me, when the vampire overseer had been far more welcoming than she ever had. Even when his emotions were as warm as an iceberg.

When Rene wasn't emotional, he was at least civil. Ursula used threats and power to coerce her subjects into doing her bidding. Rene had fought for the right to be overseer, and the majority of his people respected him. Yes, they feared his power, but he didn't abuse it, and I felt he was far stronger than any of them realized.

We exited the limo as soon as it pulled up to the mansion, and Rene led me back to the foyer. It was abuzz with activity, like a hive that had been kicked.

Many vampires who had avoided my gaze now looked at me with open appreciation.

"What is going on?" I asked.

Dimitri approached us, and I forced a smile to my face. Cass didn't bother.

He nodded to me. "The clan is excited about this new pool. We rarely get to bet on witch-related matters. But Ursula's indiscretion raises certain issues. I am concerned about Raven's safety."

"Why?" I asked before I realized he was speaking to Rene.

Dimitri clasped his hands together and I could tell it was difficult for him to address me as an equal. He and the clan were just beginning to realize how important I was to Rene. "Ursula and her coven are trying to manipulate the clan. She wanted to use you. Her mistake will cost her, and I like having the advantage. Of course, she could simply try to kill you as she has in the past and that would alleviate this mistake. We should take extra precautions. Davon has returned, and I have asked him to personally watch out for Raven. He has always been good with the newest members of our clan."

Cass frowned and Rene looked like he was frozen in place. "Who is Davon?"

Cass folded her arms. "He is Dimitri's brother. Be wary of him."

Dimitri sighed. "Davon would never hurt anyone."

Cass grunted. "I'm not worrying about him hurting her. I'm worried he will try to get in her pants. Your brother is a notorious flirt and not super discreet in that area."

Dimitri glanced away. "We all go through certain stages of development. Especially those of us who are immortal."

Cass grunted. "He is almost as old as you are. He should have sowed his oats by now."

Dimitri had an almost-defeated look, which was rare, and I had to think he wished his brother were more like him. That, of course, made me curious. "I'd like to meet him."

Rene moved closer to me. The shift of position was subtle, and Dimitri smiled. He held up his hand and motioned to a group of men in the corner of the parlor.

I noticed the resemblance as soon as the young man in a pristine dark-blue suit approached us. His dark hair and eyes were identical to Dmitri's, but he had a warm smile, and he held a crystal tumbler in his hand. His pink tie had a cartoon character on it, and I loved the mix of couture and whimsy.

He stopped beside his brother and looked Cass over suggestively. "You are looking as fine as ever, Cassara. When are you going to give a lowly vampire a chance?"

She grunted. "When pigs fly. I am not your type, Davon."

He winked at me. "You can't blame a man for trying." He held his hand out to me. "It's a pleasure to meet you, Raven. I've heard a lot about you."

"None of it good, I'm sure."

He kissed my hand gently and Rene pulled me against him. "I disagree. The clan gets a little too stagnant, if you ask me. You have made life a lot more interesting. I bet that Ursula will call Rene at six in the morning."

Cass nodded. "That's a good bet. Gives her time to have a bad night's sleep over it and catch Rene before he retires for the day."

I stared at Davon. "Are you a member of Shadow Bone?"

Dimitri nodded. "He was visiting another clan. It is the reason he was not at your introduction ball, Raven."

Davon took a sip of his drink. "Had I known there would be

so much strife as a result of your integration, I would have returned sooner."

Dimitri smoothed his tie. "That is hardly seemly."

Davon shrugged. "True though. This place has the frivolity of the Alaskan tundra at times."

Cass bit her lip to stop from smiling. "How long have you been back, Davon?"

He raised his glass to his brother. "I have been back a week, but I have been... getting acquainted with my clan members."

Dimitri huffed. "The female ones."

Davon smiled. "Women make this world worth living in, Dimitri. If you could pull your head out of your ass once in a while, you might see that."

I pursed my lips to stop from laughing. I never expected to like anything with the last name Galloway, but Davon was the complete opposite of his brother. I would take a harmless playboy over a vampire with political aspirations, any day. At least you knew what a ladies' man was after.

Dimitri glanced away in irritation before turning to Rene. "May we have a word in private?"

Cass glanced at the hallway. "I need to check in with my team. Rene, are you staying in the parlor?"

Rene touched my back. "Stay here with Davon. I will just move to the corner to speak with Dimitri."

Dimitri huffed. "She is safe within these walls. Almost the entire clan has returned and there are no off-site visits without supervision during protective protocols."

Rene stared at Dimitri for several seconds. "You seem to have forgotten that Marie was on site when she was killed. I trust no one with Raven's safety. She will remain in my line of sight, no matter where we are."

Dimitri's lips pursed. "Of course." He followed Rene when

the overseer walked toward the corner of the room, passing several clusters of well-dressed vampires.

The room was alive with chatter, and I had to wonder if I was the topic of conversation.

"It isn't that you're a witch," Davon said.

I turned to stare at him. "Pardon me?"

He motioned to the vampires surrounding us. "They don't fear you because you have magic. They fear you because your existence threatens their view of the world. Don't let it get you down."

"That obvious, huh?"

He bumped my shoulder playfully. "I hear that Isra Nassir is one of your best friends. I love Club Spice. Very entertaining."

I laughed. "I'm sure the ladies love you there."

He winked. "They do, but I only go for the shows."

"Isra is also my daughter's father."

He arched an eyebrow. "It takes a very sensual woman to convince a gay man to... experiment. I have met Isra. There isn't a heterosexual bone in his body."

I laughed. "You are so right. We had both lost people and had a brief sexual relationship." I didn't usually divulge my past so quickly, but I found my lips moving before I considered the consequences. Davon was endearing, fun, and had kind eyes. I liked him and I could see why he was popular with the ladies. He didn't strike me as the kind of man to lead you on. Nobody who shared his bed expected it to be permanent or the relationship to be monogamous.

He nodded. "Grief messes with you. Dimitri never really recovered from our parents' death or the unfortunate chain of events after. He comes across as pretty stiff, but you will learn not to take him too seriously. I don't."

"Your parents were killed? Was it vampires?"

Davon shook his head. "They were vampires and a rogue

witch killed them just after I was turned. She had fire magic and vampires are not flame retardant. There hasn't been a witch with fire magic since to my knowledge, so there is that, but I am not a super fan of the empowered." He winked. "Present company excluded."

Part of me wanted to be honest and tell him I had just learned I possessed that magic, but honestly, I had no idea how to call on it. The tests forced certain magics to the surface, but that didn't mean a witch would learn to harness their power. My fire magic could be a minor ability that produced no more than a lighter of flame when not fed by the coven's magic. "I am sorry about your parents and the coven is not exactly my friend anymore."

"Yeah, they get all uppity when you don't obey them. It's the reason I hate politics. So boring. Who wants those responsibilities, anyway?"

Davon reminded me of Isra in some ways. Jana would love him but knowing his fondness for women, there was no way I was introducing him anytime soon.

Cass strolled up to us. "Davon, I hope you are playing nice?"

He winked at her. "I would love to play with you, but you keep turning me down."

Her hand strayed to the silver staff at her belt. "I'm too much woman for you, honey. Run along. I need to speak with Raven."

Davon shook my hand again. "It was a pleasure meeting you, Raven. I hope we can spend more time together in the future." He bowed respectfully to Cass and sauntered off before striking up a conversation with a tall blond woman in a long red dress.

I stared at him for a few seconds. "Okay, I gotta say it. Davon is not what I expected."

Cass grunted. "Be careful Raven. He isn't the most... stable among us."

I turned back to her. "He hurts people?"

She shook her head. "No, not physically. Just don't count on him for... anything. He loves the ladies, but he is unreliable when it comes to anything of real importance."

"He did say he hates politics."

"That is true. It's his one redeeming quality. He prefers to party, and he isn't all that discreet about it. Protective protocols are going to put a major crimp in his lifestyle."

There were several gasps, and we turned to see Quinn making his way toward us. His stony exterior belayed his mood and clan members began to move out of his way quickly.

"What is it?" Cass asked as soon as he stopped before her.

"There has been another death."

Cassara's face mirrored Quinn's. "Where?"

"It's Sergei," he hissed.

"Who is Sergei?" I asked.

Cassara's eyes flickered. "He is our blacksmith. He makes most of our weapons."

I noticed Val speaking to Rene before his eyes blazed and he began to walk toward us. He took my hand and pulled me after him. "We are heading to the forge."

I had to jog to keep up with him, and once outside, he veered to the left of the property before taking a side trail covered in shrubs.

The silence was overpowering as we navigated the shadowy trails of the clan's property. The air was as thick as the incoming fog as I followed Rene.

It was impossible to see which way we were going, but the overseer had made this trek hundreds of times and knew the property by heart. This Sergei was obviously well-liked, and the death dealers were a hair's breadth from violence.

Rene strode through the woods with a commanding presence, and even the animals who took refuge on his property seemed to recognize his authority. The entire forest held its breath as we ventured deeper into the heart of the Shadow Bone property.

The moonlight filtered through the branches, creating flickers of light above our heads as we passed beneath them, and the distant hoot of an owl added an eerie warning to the intensity of the atmosphere.

I noticed the amber light through the trees, as well as the scent of metal and soot on the breeze. The trail opened up to reveal the workshop from another era.

CHAPTER 4

a s we approached the exterior of the forge on the clan's property, I felt a rush of trepidation, knowing what we would find inside mingled with a sense of awe. The large stone building transported me to another era, and the swaying trees surrounding the ancient structure reminded me of a time when craftsmanship and dedication were valued above all else. The forge stood like a guardian of tradition, its weathered façade regaling countless stories whispered by the wind. It was beautiful in an industrial sort of way.

The building itself was a testament to a bygone era. Its timeworn walls were composed of pitted stone and timber. Both bore the scars of years beneath a hot sun and vicious storms. The rich scent of aged wood hung in the air, mingling with the smoldering embers from within. Vines crept gracefully along the edges, as if nature itself sought to pay homage to the craftsmanship, but there were signs the natural foliage had been cut back recently.

The entrance was framed by an intricately-carved wooden door. It enticed me to step into a world where the clang of metal against metal and the rhythmic hammering of skilled hands echoed through time. But the lack of sound reminded me why we were here, and I wondered if this sacred smithy would be silent forever. There was a unique symbol branded into the wood above the door. It was worn but represented the legacy of the man within.

Small, square windows punctuated the walls, allowing flickers of amber to illuminate the night. It gave the impression of glowing eyes in the middle of the woods, as if the forge's fiery heart burned with a fierce intensity. I could see only a single overgrown road and assumed that it was a supply trail and nothing more, but there were no vehicles in the area. The moon cast an enigmatic aura, caressing the edges of the ancient stones, in contrast with the surrounding woods.

The forge itself appeared as a centerpiece of this ancient sanctuary, and was a marvel to behold. It was surrounded by the quiet majesty of nature and made me curious about the long history of our clan. It carried a legacy of those who traveled this path before, and reminded me I had the potential to forge my own way, just like the skilled artisans who once harnessed the flames in the majestic building before me. I hadn't met the blacksmith and now, I never would, but I would find his killer and help set things right for the clan he worked so diligently for.

Rene led me silently to the large wooden door before I stepped into a room that felt suspended in time, a plethora of traditions amidst the modern world. The air inside was thick with the scent of burning wood and the faint tang of metal. The quiet was interrupted by the subtle breeze as if it mourned for the loss of the immortal blacksmith.

The interior was a throwback in history. The stone walls, chiseled by hands long gone from the world, exuded a unique coolness that contrasted with the warmth radiating from the smithy. Moonlight streamed through small, wood-framed windows, casting white streams onto the worn wooden floor. The glowing centerpiece of the room was the forge itself. Like an eternal entity, it blazed with a fierce, primal energy. The lava-like heart, a cauldron of fire that danced and crackled, sending flickers of light over the room and emitting a steady warmth. The sturdy anvil sat as a sentinel of production and bore the marks of countless creations. Every strike of the blacksmith's hammer left an indelible imprint on both the metal and the soul of the forge.

Tools of various shapes and sizes hung on the stone walls. They were all meticulously organized, as were the racks of weapons stacked next to the forge. There was a small table with tongs, hammers, and chisels. The implements of the blacksmith had been used countless times and were marked with subtle scars.

There were shelves lining the smithy. They held jars of vibrant pigments, precious minerals, and intricate molds that hinted at the multifaceted nature of the blacksmith's work. There were pieces in various stages of completion on a large table, revealing the alchemy that transformed raw materials into masterpieces.

My eyes roamed around the room of wonders. "Who was this guy?"

Rene sighed. "Sergei was revered for his mastery and has trained several of our current blacksmiths."

Cass swore under her breath. "Thorin will go ballistic. If he weren't in Moscow training another apprentice, he would be down here hunting for the killer."

Rene shook his head. "Thorin must adhere to protective protocols. I allowed him to stay in Moscow to continue the apprenticeship, but if he leaves Shadow Ghost, then he will be remanded to his own clan."

I frowned. "Who is Thorin and what clan does he belong to?"

"Thorin is our oldest weapons master. He trained Sergei and is as good with a sword as Constantine, but prefers to create rather than fight. He is a member of Shadow Phantom, but he has a skilled apprentice in his home clan and has been in Moscow for the last forty years, training another apprentice."

Cass led us to the man lying on the floor by the forge. The blacksmith, a figure that seemed to belong to another era, was frozen in a moment of vulnerability and strength. His stone skin was similar to the very walls he was entombed in, and I hated the end that had befallen the diligent craftsman. The air was heavy, as if time itself had conspired to cast a veil over the grisly scene.

His form was sprawled out amidst the tools and debris of the forge, like an unlikely tableau. His brown leather clothes and apron bore the smudges of labor, and his hands were calloused and scarred. They spoke of a life lived through the heat of the flames and the rhythm of the hammer's dance. One that had endured since his time as a human. Vampires did not display such symptoms of hard labor unless they occurred prior to transition. His face was serene despite the circumstances, as if he had given his all to the craft that he loved.

The forge seemed to be watching over him. Its fiery heart having been the source of both his creations and his victories. The hearth was cooling but still bore the marks of its fiery dance. The tools that surrounded him, each meticulously cared for and imbued with history, spoke of a devotion that went beyond mere craftsmanship. A monument to man and his art.

"This is a travesty," Quinn whispered.

I glanced at the array of weapons on the shelves and hung on the walls. "He made all the weapons in the training facility, didn't he?"

Cass nodded. "We also have an armory, but it is locked down unless we are at war. The silver spears utilized by the seniors were before Sergei's time, but he made the rest."

I looked for a velvet pouch, but there was nothing on any of the tables near the body. "How was he infected?"

We all moved to various shelves and weapons, but none of us

could find any hint of the deadly compound that turned the vampires to stone.

Cass stood with a cell phone she picked up from underneath one of the shelves. It looked completely out of place in the room, but then so did we. "He dropped his phone. Maybe he was trying to..." She opened the screen and hissed.

"What is it?" Quinn asked.

"Traitor in the woods. That's what he typed before he dropped the phone."

Quinn knelt down beside Cass. "If he saw who it was, he would've told us. He's an older vampire. Perhaps he was infected outside, and that's why we can't find a velvet pouch. He made it back to the forge before he died. Sergei hated technology, so the phone would've been inside if he were checking the surrounding area."

Cass stood. "Let's check the woods. If he was infected outside, he didn't have a lot of time to make it back here. The source of the attack has to be close."

We exited the smithy in silence. Rene pointed in several directions. "Raven will stay with me. Fan out and search the surrounding area. There are multiple sets of tracks, but Sergei liked to walk the woods when a new weapon was cooling."

We each chose a set of tracks leading from the forge, though once inside the dense woods, I couldn't see any sign of anyone wandering through the foliage.

Rene appeared to see something that I did not, as he pulled me along as he passed several young trees, reaching for the heavens. Pine needles rushed against my clothes and the earthy scent of the breeze was refreshingly soothing.

Quinn shouted and Rene turned toward the sound, leading me through the forest as if he did daily treks in the overgrown area.

I was expecting to find a scuffle or some other signs of a fight when we exited the brush, but Cass stood beside her death dealer, looking down at the strange garden that shouldn't exist in the forest.

Rene glanced at the manicured foliage. "What is this?"

Cass shrugged. "I have no idea. If this were a human property, I would say it's a grow op but I don't recognize the plants."

I released Rene's hand to walk around the garden. Several plants were familiar and hardly rare, but one was the complete opposite. "That is Star Canyon. The seeds are extremely rare. The high priestess had me growing them for the coven when I was human. Well, when I was still an owner of Powerful Petals."

"Why would it be here? What does this plant do?"

My eyes roamed over the area full of plants. Individually they were harmless, but as my mind added each ingredient together, my hand went to my mouth. "Oh, no."

Rene moved, so he was next to me. "What is it? What do these plants do when combined?"

My eyes met his. "I think we are looking at the ingredients for the compound that turns vampires to stone."

Rene's eyes flickered with red. "A traitor in our clan is growing the necessary ingredients on our property?"

I nodded. "The other plants are common, but Star Canyon is extremely difficult to source. Honestly, I thought that you needed to be a member of the coven to get seeds in this quantity."

"You suspect Ursula?" Rene asked.

"I don't know anyone else who could get their hands on the seeds needed to create this garden. Unless there is another supplier I am unaware of. I heard there are some black-market seeds, but these plants are of the highest quality." I motioned to the forest. "This isn't an ideal location to grow the plant. They need more sunlight, so I'm guessing that a witch with similar magic to mine is... encouraging the plants to grow in less-than-optimal conditions."

Rene growled. "This traitor has access to security measures. How else would he keep this hidden?"

I shrugged. "It could be a woman."

Cass shook her head. "I am the only female in Shadow Bone with access to all aspects of security. It has to be a senior in the clan."

Quinn rubbed his chin. "It could be an aide. The seniors all have one. They give their aide access to their information to perform daily tasks."

"Is an aide like a secretary?" I asked.

Cass nodded. "Basically. All the seniors have one, but they are fully vetted. We are diligent about security. Though I never believed any vampire would conspire with a witch."

"Excuse me?"

Cass sighed. "I don't mean you, honey. You aren't a witch to me. You are an empowered vampire."

"Isn't that the same thing?"

Rene shook his head. "No. You have shown no loyalty to your coven, and with good reason. They had every chance to secure your favor, but treated you as a second-class citizen when they should have cherished you. I will not make the same mistake."

I felt a twinge of regret at his words. Part of me still wanted the coven to accept the woman I was when I was alive. That moment had passed and there was no future for me with my empowered sisters. "You are right, and I do appreciate all you have done for me. It's easy to forget that I am just as unusual in your world as I am in the coven's."

Cass grabbed her phone when it rang. "Hey, Manu." Her voice lacked the enthusiasm it usually held when speaking with the antiquities dealer.

Her eyes snapped to Rene. "Manu found something. He thinks he may know where the next page of the prophecy is."

Rene glanced around the forest. "Quinn station someone at

this garden going forward, but have them stay hidden. I want to know who comes to visit this location."

Quinn moved away to make arrangements as Rene turned back to Cass.

"Ask Manu if the page is in Shadow Bone territory."

She nodded. "He thinks he has narrowed down the location, though."

"Tell him to meet us in the conference room. We will be there shortly."

Cass relayed the information as we started walking back to the mansion. The silence was interrupted by the thud of my boots on the fallen branches, but neither Rene nor Cass made a sound.

I ignored the hushed glances and trepid stares as we entered the foyer. While the clan may not know who had been killed, they were aware something awful had happened and likely had an idea that another vamp was murdered.

Manu was sitting at the long table and his head snapped up as we entered. "This is very exciting." He turned the scroll he was reading around and pointed to a passage as Cass neared him.

Rene and Cass stared at it, but I was unable to read the script. "What does it say?"

Rene frowned. "Manu has found a scroll pertaining to Magda. This suggests she did not have magic but some kind of human abilities. Different from that of the witches. They call her a... gypsy. For lack of a modern translation."

"She had the same ability I do. The mental thing."

Rene nodded. "That is my guess. There is no way to be sure unless we follow her instructions."

"What instructions?" I asked.

Rene pointed to the scroll. "She wrote this, and it says she hid the page located on Shadow Bone property herself. It appears she was quite adept at fooling those around her regarding her skill, and I assume she had the ability to connect with them in some way. Perhaps her gift was stronger than yours and she could... influence anyone she came in contact with. We have instructions, but not a starting point. Manu has further work to do."

I shivered. "She could control people's minds. That's a scary thought."

Rene nodded. "It is. I would like to discuss the gift you possessed in life with Jana, since you no longer have the ability."

My eyes widened. "You think Jana has it?"

"Possibly. But we need to know either way. Even if she doesn't, she may have an insight that we no longer possess."

I sighed as Manu and Cass stared at me. "Okay. I will call her."

CHAPTER 5

We waited till the early hours of the morning. Before I called Jana. I wasn't surprised I had woken her and if it wasn't so important, I wouldn't have, but she had been happy to hear from me and promised to come over in half an hour.

Rene and I were waiting by the front door, speaking quietly. As I stood in the opulence of the foyer, surrounded by my fellow vampires, the air was heavy with tension and mistrust. A serial killer had that effect on people, including the immortal ones. The atmosphere crackled like a lightning storm, and I could practically taste the resentment in the air. Every sideways glance, and subtle curl of their lips, whispered the one truth that I couldn't ignore— they didn't trust me. They blamed me for the events that had befallen them.

At my age, I'd faced my share of challenges and adversities in life, but being an outsider in a clan of vampires was an entirely different battle. I expected their skepticism. Of me and my intentions. It was as if they could detect the uncertainty that lingered in my mind. That I was the source of their woes.

The way they exchanged whispered words that I couldn't

decipher only fueled my anxiety. It was obvious they had formed a tight-knit bond over the years. One my appearance threatened to shatter. This wasn't about trust; it was about power and envy. My proximity to Rene rubbed those with significant clan stature the wrong way.

Their eyes bored into my back, tracing my every move, and dissecting every nuance of my expression. It wasn't just my presence that troubled them; it was Rene's interest in me. Jealousy simmered beneath their frosty exteriors, a potent mix of resentment and longing. Frustration tangled with determination, as I waited for the one person who lightened my soul like no other.

When Rene opened the door to allow her entry into the foyer, my heart leaped. It had done the same thing when I laid eyes on her for the first time and my excitement at being in Jana's presence had only grown over the years.

Jana was the epitome of youthful beauty, with her radiant smile and shiny, black hair that seemed to catch every flicker of light. I wasn't sure how I felt about the appreciative stares she received while at the clan. The male members' eyes seemed to linger a little too long for my taste. In their eyes, Jana was a beacon of charm and innocence.

Still, as Jana ignored the attentive stares, I felt a certain pride. She was my legacy, my child, and watching her embrace her own power was a testament to her strength and the values Isra and I had instilled in her.

I hugged her fiercely when she wrapped her arms around me. "Thanks for coming. Sorry I woke you."

She waved her hand negligently. "I will sleep when I am dead. It sounded urgent... sorry about the dead comment."

Rene made a barely perceptible motion with his hand and the men admiring my daughter turned away and continued their conversations with their group.

Rene smiled warmly at Jana. "I assure you, it is fine. Thank you for coming, Miss Nasir."

Jana winked at him. "You are cute when you are formal."

There were some hushed chuckles around the room as Rene motioned toward the stairs. "Will you accompany Raven and I to our suite?"

We ascended the lavish staircase, and I had to admire how Jana could be so comfortable wearing simple jeans and a T-shirt when the surrounding vampires were in haute couture. Of course, she was used to drag queen attire.

I walked beside her as Rene trailed behind us. There was a hushed silence, and I glanced back to see everyone looking at me.

"What is that about?" Jana asked.

"I don't know. They have some odd protocols, and I probably broke one."

Jana bumped my shoulder. "Then good on you. They seem a little too rigid. They need to live a little."

I pursed my lips.

Jana gave me a withered look. "I just realized how ridiculous that sounded, but I mean that in the proverbial sense."

"I get it, honey. It is accurate, though."

We walked in silence until we entered the suite. I led Jana to the large office, and we took a seat on the couch. Rene took the chair opposite us and crossed his legs after he sat. He looked like he was there for a friendly visit and no tension was reflected in his gaze, but I could sense his eagerness to learn more about my strange ability.

"Jana, I asked your mother to call you here so I could ask you about your telepathic connection."

Jana stiffened on the couch next to me and I felt like I had betrayed her. I had asked her to keep that strange connection a secret and now a vampire she barely knew asking her about it.

I touched her arm. "I'm sorry, honey. It appears there was a vampire fifteen hundred years ago who had a similar ability in life. We are wondering if there is a connection to me turning successfully."

She frowned as glanced between me and Rene. "What would that have to do with being a witch?"

Rene shrugged casually. "I believe it is a human ability and has nothing to do with magical power. You have no magic, but you can create this connection with your mother."

Jana nibbled her lip. "I am pretty sure Mom creates the connection. She seems to know when I need it, but it hasn't happened a lot or anything."

Rene nodded. "While your mother's gift is likely stronger than yours, you must have some level of ability. May I ask if you remember the first time it happened?"

Jana was quiet for a moment. "Mom told me about the incident when I was a toddler, but I don't remember that. When I was ten, I was swimming, and I swam underneath the wharf, despite my parents telling me not to, when we were at the lake. I bumped my head and began to panic, but Mom invaded my mind and... commanded me not to panic. She told me to swim down a bit and resurface outside the dock, and I did. She was already swimming toward me when I got on top. I had a goose egg the size of Mars, but it could have been a lot worse."

My heart squeezed a little at the memory. "I was so freaked out by that incident. I don't think I let you out of my sight for six months."

Jana nodded. "I could feel you checking on me when I was in class. I guess I am never really away from you."

I frowned. "I don't have the ability anymore, honey."

Jana's eyebrows furrowed. "Really? It was always kind of comforting to know you would come if I called you."

Rene shifted in his seat slightly. "I am not convinced that

Raven won't regain her abilities. It is too soon after her transition to make such assumptions. Vampires develop over decades, not weeks."

Jana sighed. "I could be eighty before Mom regains it though."

The slight blip of fear that squeezed my heart earlier was nothing compared to the twisting in my core at the thought of me outliving Jana.

Rene glanced at me, but his face remained stoic. "I hope you will consider testing when you are ready. But you are a part of my family, no matter what you decide."

Rene's statement helped ease the tension in my core. But this predicament was why vampires were vetted and their family dynamic weighed upon before approval. Unfortunately, I knew the truth about Jana. "She doesn't want to be a vampire, Rene. I didn't either, so I have to accept the consequences of these events... someday." I heard the pain in my voice. So did Rene and Jana. There was a good chance I would follow my daughter when she left this world. I could handle her aging, but not dying.

Jana was quiet for some time. "I want to talk about that, but let's focus on why you think Mom's telepathic ability is somehow responsible for her transition."

Rene was staring at me. "I can't confirm it is. Raven, when did you begin to... sense things?"

I never thought about the strange ability I had. "I don't remember a time when I didn't. It was more of a sixth-sense thing when I was younger. Nothing overt and everything I did was easily explained, so nobody ever noticed it... well, until Jana."

"Your mother did not have this ability?" Rene asked.

"No. The earliest... occurrence was when I was eight. My mom was cooking pasta, and she had an apron on. It came undone and caught on the pot handle. Seconds before she would have pulled the boiling water onto herself, I yanked her out of the way.

The pot hit the floor, and she still got a minor burn through her pants, but it could have been a lot worse if that water hit her arms."

"That could have been passed off as instinct. Not... premonition."

"It was. I assumed I saw what was about to happen, but I was in the other room and had to rush to the kitchen."

"You realize what you are describing differs from what you did with Jana. You did not command your mother. You simply sensed danger."

I shrugged. "Maybe my gift developed over time, too. I was a child then. And in every instance, my connection was with a family member. I have never been able to avert an accident for Isra, and I love him."

Rene's jaw twitched. "You never attempted to develop this ability, so it is impossible to say whether you could have learned to connect to those around you."

I shrugged. "Nothing showed in the witch testing, so there wasn't anyone to help train me. I didn't recognize it as anything special. Even when I connected with Jana, and I was happy that I did, part of me felt more alone than ever. Like I was some kind of mutant."

Jana's eyes widened. "No way. You are amazing. I can't believe you said that. Or felt that way. It was the complete opposite for me. I felt like we were superheroes keeping our identity secret."

I arched an eyebrow. "Superheroes. Really?"

Jana laughed. "Give me a break. I was a kid."

"Thank you for telling me. I am sorry I lost it now."

Jana tapped her chin with her finger. "I wonder if I will develop the ability in time. Where I can connect with and not the other way around. I do sense things sometimes."

I leaned toward her. "You do?"

She nodded. "You never liked discussing our ability. So I never bring it up, but I had an incident two months ago where I was sure Dad was going to fall on the stairs to the stage. He was wearing his five-inch platforms, and I insisted on walking him up."

"Did he fall?" I asked.

"He slipped, but I stopped him from tumbling. Those shoes have mysteriously disappeared from his wardrobe."

"He threw them away?" I asked,

Jana gave me her classic "Are you kidding me?" look. "Please. Those were two-thousand-dollar boots. I sold them online and gave him the money."

"He wasn't mad?"

"He already had his eye on a replacement, and they were far more stable."

Rene stood up. "May I offer you a glass of orange juice, Jana?"

She blinked. "You have human food in the suite?"

Rene motioned to a full fridge in the corner. I hadn't even noticed the new addition when we walked in. "I will have all yours and your father's... favorite foods on hand at all times."

I had to blink away the tears that formed in my eyes as Rene moved to the fridge. "Thank you, Rene."

He nodded to me respectfully. "Would you like a cranberry scone with your juice?"

Jana's jaw dropped. "That is awfully specific. How did you know that's my favorite?"

Rene smiled as he grabbed the orange juice from the fridge. "It was simple. I asked your father. He provided me with a list of... staples."

Jana laughed. "I should have known. He plans to exploit his connection to you like a fly on shit when you marry my mom."

I coughed as Rene paused in the process of pouring the juice.

"Jana, that is highly inappropriate. Isra has no right to say things like that."

Jana folded her arms and gave me a defiant look. "Is that true, Rene?"

Rene continued to pour her juice and grabbed a scone. "It is my hope that your father will be able to... exploit me in the future, yes."

Jana smiled as my jaw dropped. "Rene, I like you more every time I see you."

Rene returned to the couch and placed the scone in front of Jana before handing her the orange juice. "The feeling is mutual."

"Are you two nuts?" I asked in an exasperated tone. Part of me was horrified, but if I was honest, another part sizzled with excitement.

Jana chuckled. "You have your work cut out for you, Rene."

He sat back down in his chair. "I am aware. But I assure you I am up to the challenge."

I fidgeted with my fingers. "If you two would stop conspiring against me, I would like to discuss your earlier comment about becoming a vampire."

Jana took a long swig of her juice. "You just want to change the subject."

"Yes." I gave her my stern voice. One I used when she was younger and trying to change my mind about a parental decision.

"Fair enough. My mom is a witch and I have heard the stories of witch transitions. The ones about witches who died with vampire venom in their blood. They were pretty gruesome."

Rene nodded. "They are and they are true. The early attempts to turn a witch were horrifying. There have been few deaths in the last thousand years, but I have seen firsthand the pain an empowered person endures in an attempt to transition."

Jana finished her juice and placed the glass on the table. "I'm not into pain. That was the true reason I didn't want to attempt transition. With Mom being a witch, I assumed I would not be compatible."

"We can no longer assume that is true. I would ask you to consider waiting until you have found a partner and had children, if that is your wish."

I pursed my lips, as the thought of grandchildren hadn't really hit my radar. I wanted my daughter for eternity and hadn't considered that aspect of her life. It just hadn't been something we discussed. She was too young and hadn't had a serious relationship yet.

Jana nodded. "I am not sure about that. I would consider taking the tests, though. Just so I know what my options are, but I want it understood that it is my decision."

"Of course," Rene said.

She grabbed her scone and took a small bite. "You should get a small microwave. These are better warmed up."

Rene nodded. "It will be here for your next visit."

Jana was staring at her food, but I could tell her mind was not on the food. "I never really looked into the vampire thing. Is there an information packet? I would like to understand the process."

Rene took out his phone and typed into it. "I have asked our admissions counselor to send you everything and have informed her that I will be sponsoring you if you choose to join our clan."

"Would I be your daughter? I mean, in the clan sense."

Rene's head cocked to the side. "You already are Jana. I have chosen your mother. Whether she chooses me does not change that."

Jana chewed her scone quickly and coughed when she swallowed. "Wow. You don't pull any punches do you, Rene?"

"I have lived through enough heartache and deception for ten lifetimes. I prefer honesty and loyalty in such things."

Jana stared at him. "Those things are important, but not as much as love. I would rather have one lifetime full of unconditional love than ten with mere honesty. And despite her predicament, so would my mom."

My daughter hadn't surprised me in a long time. I knew the straightforward woman I had raised, but her ability to cut to the heart of an issue without backing down was awe-inspiring. Especially when she was putting the most powerful creature in the world on the spot.

Rene arched an eyebrow and, while I expected him to be irritated, he looked intrigued. "I couldn't agree with you more, Jana. And the fact that you have asked this question confirms I must double my efforts to persuade your mother and you of my intentions."

Jana nodded. "You probably wanted to give her time to adjust, but if you give her too much, you won't convince her you are serious."

Rene's eyes flickered red. "I assure you I have never been more... serious about anything in my life."

Jana took another bite of her scone and leaned toward me. "You are in so much trouble."

"Thanks to you," I said, but my mind was racing. Rene had answered every question my daughter posed. Was it that simple? "Jana, how is your dad and the club?"

Jana finished her scone. "He is good. Getting blisters from the new boots, but that's expected. He has a new couture gown on order and is training Max. That young man has the voice of an angel, but his act needs some work. He could be a headliner someday."

"I am glad he took him in. He lost everyone he loved. He will thrive at Club Spice with the other ladies."

"He will. Max is grateful for the opportunity and really puts the work in. Dad is looking to find him a small apartment, but his van is parked at the club for now."

"Maybe you could rent him a room at the house. You barely

stay there anymore," I said absently as my mind was more focused on Rene's words than Jana's.

She pursed her lips. "I was thinking the same thing. But I wasn't sure the house was mine to make that decision."

I grabbed her hand. "Everything I have is yours. I just want to pick up a few personal items I left when Cass and I were there last, but I don't need a room at the house. I would stay with Isra if needed."

"That will not be necessary," Rene said. His voice was neutral, but I detected his irritation.

Jana smiled. "Oh, yeah. You are in trouble. "

I shook my head. "Rent the house or part of it. Whatever you want. I will arrange to pick up my things."

Rene typed into his phone. "They will be retrieved tomorrow."

Jana stood. "I have to go. Max and I are going to yoga in an hour, and I want to grab a few things."

I arched an eyebrow. "You have become friends with him?"

She nodded. "Yeah. He wrote me a song. It's hard to explain. But I really care for him. As a friend."

"I know what you mean. Isra and I had that connection from the moment we met."

"Well, I'm not having babies with him, if that is what you are thinking. I love my life and my dad, but I do want a more conventional relationship. No offense."

"None taken. I want you to be happy."

Rene stood. "May we walk you out, Jana?"

She nodded, but as we approached the door, Rene's phone beeped. He glanced at the screen. "That was Manu. He found something he wishes me to look at."

CHAPTER 6

*M*any of the men in the foyer glanced at my daughter as we escorted her to the main entrance of the mansion. There were fewer clan members gathered in the grand foyer as it was less than an hour from dawn. Even though many vampires didn't require much sleep, they tended to retire to their rooms during the day for quiet activities.

Jana gave me a quick hug before she slipped through the door. Her car was sitting at the end of the canopy, and I waited till she got in before I turned to Rene.

"Are we meeting Manu in the conference room?"

Rene nodded and placed his hand on my back as he led me through the foyer to the hallway. We passed several distinguished-looking portraits in the hall before I stopped in front of one of them.

In the dimly-lit hallway, I found myself drawn to a portrait hanging on the wall, a perfect replica from a bygone era. My gaze locked onto the image of an older man, whose presence seemed to emanate from the canvas itself. I knew he was a vampire by the otherworldly gaze in his eyes. Years that had passed since he walked the earth, but it hadn't dulled the intensity of his painting.

His eyes seemed to cut into an onlooker's soul, as if he were whispering secrets only a vampire understood. They were a shade of indigo and held mysteries as ancient as time itself. They conveyed his life experiences. Both the joys and sorrows of a life that had spanned centuries.

His face was a medley of sharp angles and soft curves. A timeless embodiment of both danger and charisma. His pale skin, a porcelain canvas, was a stark contrast to the rich darkness of his hair cascading in untamed waves over his shoulders. The moonlight filtering through the chamber he sat in during the portrait's creation seemed to kiss his features, highlighting the regal arch of his brows and the chiseled line of his jaw.

The clothing he wore, a medley of velvet and lace that draped his rigid torso, expressed his importance in the era in which he lived. A high-collared red cloak billowed behind him, adding an air of mystery and a hint of the supernatural. As my eyes roamed over his attire, I imagined the nights when he prowled the cobbled streets, a shadow amongst shadows.

But it was his expression that held my attention—a delicate balance of sorrow and yearning, as if he had lost his connection to the light and walked in eternal darkness. His full lips held a hint of a melancholic smile, one that hinted at untold secrets.

"You must have lost a lot of people over the years. It must be hard for you to walk these halls."

Rene glanced at the painting. "Many of my brethren have passed in the last two thousand years, but Mortas was not one of them. He was the overseer prior to Siam. He was a young overseer and Siam was a skilled fighter. There are several scrolls that say Siam tricked him and his death was not true."

"I'm sure some men would use anything in their arsenal to bring down a stronger opponent."

Rene nodded. "The story suggests Mortas was entombed and

there was no true ascension, but that was thousands of years ago, and he would be long dead by now, regardless of how he was killed."

I shivered. "I hope it was a fight. Buried alive and left to die of starvation. That is about as bad as it gets."

Rene nodded. "Especially for a vampire. It could take hundreds of years for the body to fully give up in such conditions."

I placed my hand on my stomach. "That's horrible. Let's head to the conference room." We passed another young couple just before we reached our destination, and they nodded respectfully at Rene.

Manu's head popped up as we entered the conference room, and it was impossible not to detect the excitement on his face. "Rene, look at this." His shiny black hair fell in his eyes when he moved and he shook it away as he pointed to a strange scroll.

Rene moved to his side of the long table so he could read the scroll Manu had unfurled on the table. "That is the last will and testament of Count Vladir. He was a clan head when Siam was the overseer, but became an author after his duties ended. I liked him. He died fifteen hundred years ago."

Manu rubbed his chin. "How did he die, Rene?"

"He was murdered. I assumed it was a monster hunter. They were still active at that time in our history."

"Maybe, but look at the scroll next to the light." He stood and placed the ancient parchment in front of a wall sconce.

Rene leaned forward as a small mark appeared. "That is a witch's mark. Specifically, Magda's. What is it doing here and how was it imbued in the scroll?"

I recognized the spell. It wasn't powerful, and most witches of power could easily perform such a feat. "Magic. A witch added the mark when the document was created."

Rene's eyes flickered. "How can you be sure it was at the same time? The mark could have been added after Vladir's scroll was created."

Manu shook his head. "I agree with Raven. This mark was on the paper before he wrote it. He either had contact with the witch or he was forced to leave this where a future generation would find it."

Rene's eyes narrowed. "You believe he was forced to seek his rest. Set up to die so this document would lead to him."

Manu nodded. "Which insinuates that either Magda, or another witch from that time, was working with the monster hunters."

Rene took the parchment from Manu. "The only thing left of Vladir is his portrait and his grave."

I gagged. "I am not into digging up a coffin from fifteen hundred years ago."

Rene shook his head. "That would not be necessary. He has a fairly-large mausoleum in the cemetery."

I shivered. "I hate crypts."

"It is still preferable to digging," Manu said.

Rene passed the page back to Manu. "You wish to search Vladir's crypt."

Manu smiled like a child with a new toy. "Yes. Very much so. It may not be a page, but I suspect it is."

Rene nodded. "We know there is a page on clan property and are already checking any leads regarding the prophecy. The three of us will check this one."

Manau glanced at the door. "Where is Cass?"

"She has some personal business to attend to," he said.

Manu rolled the scroll back up and affixed the twine, before placing it on the shelf. "I'm ready. Lead the way."

Rene took my hand and led me from the conference room as Manu followed.

I lowered my voice and leaned toward him slightly. "What is Cass doing?"

Rene and I passed several couples in the hallway as we reached the parlor. "She is training her younger members." It was Cassara's job to train the death dealers, and while there was no inflection in Rene's voice, I had a feeling there was more to it.

"She is training all the younger members. Not just Kirnen?"

Rene opened the main door for me and indicated for me to exit the mansion. "She is spending some... quality time with Kirnen."

I paused outside as Manu exited. "This better not have anything to do with him sparring with me."

Rene took my hand. "Of course it does. He is talented enough that he should not have made such a mistake."

I stopped and tried to release Rene's hand, but found him reluctant to do so. "Don't hold him accountable for my mistake. His weapon could never have done any permanent damage to an immortal."

"It could have if he stabbed you in the heart," Rene said coldly.

"He didn't aim at my heart. If you want a serious relationship between us, then you can't wrap me in cotton. I have to live that undead life the best I can. If people have to step on eggshells around me, I won't make it here."

Manu stopped and stared at the overseer. He was clearly interested in Rene's response, but he remained quiet.

Rene rolled his shoulders, and it was clear he was not used to being questioned in clan matters. "I understand." It wasn't exactly an apology, or even an admission of guilt, but I understood he was unused to changing his mind about a decision.

Manu winked at me when I glanced at him. I was expecting to drive to the mausoleum, but we turned left at the end of the canopy and made our way to a trail on the side of the mansion.

The wrought-iron gates of the private cemetery were intricate works of art. They were open slightly, as if welcoming their fellow clan members to visit. The cold breeze washed over me, sending shivers down my spine. I didn't have to ask which one we were visiting as Vladir's name was etched in thick bold letters above his final resting place. It was one of the oldest and grandest in the area.

His private mausoleum stood as a testament to a bygone era, but retained its grandeur after all this time. The stone walls were pitted and weathered by time, but seemed to tell a story in their own right. This was no ordinary burial site; it was a place of reverence for a vampire and was a reflection of the prestige he held within his clan.

The door scraped the stone loudly when Rene opened it and cobwebs stretched out before breaking their silky threads.

Inside, the air was a heavy mix of mustiness and antiquity as dust particles floated in the air from our intrusion. A hushed silence lingered around us, as if the walls held their breath in respect. Vines draped gracefully over the stone from a crack in the rear of the chamber, making a green latticework of the interior.

My footsteps echoed through the cool and damp air. It embraced me like a comforting presence as my eyes were drawn to the centerpiece—an ornate sarcophagus, adorned with delicate engravings that seemed to dance in the half-light. The details were exquisite, a testament to the craftsmanship of its creator.

"Where do we look first?" I asked, breaking the ancient silence.

Manu went to the vine-laced walls, sliding his hands over them. "There don't appear to be any unnatural indents. Look for anything that appears out of place and may have been added after Vladir's death."

We all inspected the walls, but after fifteen minutes, we had covered every nook and crevice without any success. I dusted the dirt from my hands.

"Any idea what to try next?"

Manu pointed to the sarcophagus. "We need to open it."

Rene's lips pursed slightly and while he said nothing, I was sure he was not thrilled with the idea of disturbing Vladir's eternal slumber. "I will breech the seal." He moved to the side of the intricately-carved sarcophagus and pushed on the top. There was a grating sound as a burst of stale air fermented the room and Vladir's body was exposed for the first time in fifteen hundred years.

The desiccated body of the ancient vampire lay inside the sarcophagus, wrapped in tattered remnants of what might have once been regal attire. The fabric clung to the fragile bones, reluctant to release its hold even after all these years.

He held a simple wooden staff in his hands and Manu gently took it from his grasp as Rene stared at the remains of the former clan member. It was a stark reminder that the undead were not truly immortal. They simply had a different life cycle than humans.

Manu inspected the thick circular piece of wood. It looked unimpressive except for a few strange symbols etched in a line. "This is it, but I am unsure how to open it. There doesn't appear to be a device."

Rene pushed the lid of the sarcophagus back in place. "How can you be sure that contains the page?"

Manu pointed at one of the symbols. "This one is on the first page. Vladir's seal is the last one in the line. There are a few I don't recognize."

Rene dusted off his hands before holding one out to Manu. "Let me see."

Manu handed the wooden baton to him. "Do you know what the other symbols are?"

Rene rolled the staff over in his hands. "One of these is the symbol for the overseer. I have not used it in over a thousand years."

"Why would you change your seal?"

Rene rolled his shoulders slightly. "I did not like what it represented."

I touched his back slightly. "What does the symbol mean?"

"Supremacy."

I arched an eyebrow. "Over the human race?"

"Over all races. It was the creed of the previous overseers. I changed it after the Lycans were destroyed. Victory is hollow when you have eradicated an entire species."

I pursed my lips. "Do you have a new seal?"

He nodded. "It is a symbol from the old language. It means harmony."

I smiled. "I like that."

"As do I." He continued to turn the staff over in his hand.

I felt a slight tingle and turned to glance outside the mausoleum. The breeze sent a leaf fluttering over the stone floor, but nothing was amiss. Still. The sensation in my chest continued to grow. "Do you feel that?"

Rene and Manu both turned to stare out the open stone slab that doubled as a door.

"I do not," Rene said.

Manu shook his head as I tried to focus on the source of the strange sensation. It took me a few seconds to ascertain it came from the wooden wand in Rene's hand. "May I see that?"

Rene handed it to me. "It's a spell. You need magic to open this. I hate to admit this, but a witch was involved in Vladir's death."

Rene pointed to the wand. "Can you break the ward around the scroll?"

I frowned. "I am not sure." As I held the etched wood in my hand, words formed in my mind.

"Ancient of the midnight sky, reveal the mystery that lies. Unveil your secrets deep and continue your endless sleep." The wand hummed in my hand before the end dissolved and a circular hole was revealed. I tipped the wand toward my hand before a scroll slid from within.

Manu put his hands out eagerly. "May I?"

CHAPTER 7

I passed the scroll to Manu, and the ancient parchment crackled slightly as he gingerly brought it closer to his face.

His eyes moved over it eagerly and his pupils dilated as they roamed over the old script. "Rene, this is remarkable. It's hard to believe this was here all this time. Just steps from the mansion."

Rene nodded. "It is ingenious, really. We would never desecrate a vampire's resting place. We take our eternal rest... quite seriously."

Manu held up the scroll and flashed his light at the edges. "Let's take this back to the conference room. We have the other pages and can see if they reveal more information when brought together."

Rene moved to the door. "I agree. Dawn is almost upon us, and I wish to have Raven inside." I stepped out of the mausoleum and though it was still dark, there was a sliver of orange on the horizon and my skin prickled. The tingly sensation bordered on pain, but I waited patiently as Manu exited behind me and Rene closed the door to the mausoleum.

We walked back to the mansion in silence, and Manu had his

eyes on the paper the entire time. He tripped on an exposed tree root and Rene grabbed him to avert him from falling.

"Thank you," Manu said absently as his eyes remained on the page.

We entered the foyer to find a trio of vampires standing by the stairs and the rest of the massive room empty. They nodded to Rene as we passed them and continued to the conference room.

Rene opened the door, and I scooted in, followed by Manu. He placed the newest page on the table, then grabbed the others from the shelf and put them together. As soon as the pieces touched one another, the lettering began to glow, and a secret passage lit up.

"What is that?" I asked.

Manu held his hands away from the pages. "I don't know. The scripture is distorted when I look at it. Perhaps a spell of some sort?"

Rene stared at the page. "It is the same for me."

I moved closer to Manu so I could stare at the writing. "That's strange. It looks fine to me."

"Read it to us," Rene said.

"When the undead witch walks the earth and the moon rises high, she will call upon the magic hidden inside. Unleash her power, make it dormant no more, bring it to the surface, and let it soar." As soon as the last word escaped my lips, my body began to heat. I released the page and touched my forehead.

"Raven, what is it?" Rene asked with concern.

"I am not sure, but I feel hot, and my skin is tingly." I backed away as a flame erupted in my palm."

"Raven?"

I flipped my palm up and down as the single flame moved over my skin without burning me. "I think this activated my fire magic, but I have no idea how to control it. My body feels like a pot about to boil over."

Manu stared at the page of the prophecy. "This passage was about Raven. She could see it because she was meant to read it. The script did something to her power. Made it more..."

Rene cursed under his breath. "She was bound. The spell released her latent magic. Her death started the process of magic regeneration, but this scroll removed any barriers left in place. I should have seen the signs."

I stared at the open flame in my hand. "You aren't a witch, Rene. You couldn't have known." The flame pulsed and engulfed my entire hand as Rene and Manu backed away from me.

Fire was one of the few ways to kill a vampire. Once the heart was incinerated, it was over for any creature, including the undead. "Can you rein your power in Raven?"

I focused on the flow of power within me, attempting to moderate the micro surges that pulsed within me.

"I am trying." The pulse felt strange, and I had read all of Magda's writings. This magic was unfamiliar. "This wasn't Magda. She could not have added this spell."

"Who was it?" Rene asked.

I concentrated on the magic I felt. It was powerful, and I had only come across one person who had that level of power. "It had to be the high priestess at the time. I am having trouble counteracting her spell."

Rene hissed. "The coven has been working on their own agenda this entire time. And it ends with the extinction of my species."

Manu frowned. "Why would they do this? Mass genocide is pretty dark, even for the coven."

Rene huffed. "They fear our evolution. The lycan king taught them that every being must eventually die. They are ensuring it happens sooner than later."

My stomach rolled at the implication of his words. "Do you think Ursula is responsible for the vampire murders?"

"Yes. As well as the multiple murder attempts on your life."

My heart squeezed, and the fire died in my hand. Apparently, complete despair was a mood killer that even my magic couldn't overcome. "Are we going to confront her?"

Rene nodded. "As soon as you rest. We will visit the coven building at dusk." He led me from the room and I walked like a wooden statue back to our suite.

I woke to Rene caressing my back. I remembered returning to the suite and him feeding me a glass of blood before removing my clothes and tucking me into bed. He sat on the side as I drifted off, and I was sure I heard him head to his office once I was close to succumbing to my slumber.

It was thoughtful of him to watch over me and I felt cared for when he should hate me for being a witch. My species was trying to eradicate him, and he held no animosity toward me. I wished I had given him the benefit of the doubt when the tables were reversed. Prior to my death, I would never have considered a vampire as anything but a plague. How ironic.

I rolled onto my back to find Rene lying on the covers in a fresh suit and I sighed in frustration.

"What is wrong, Raven?"

My hand slipped to his black silk tie, and I allowed the velvety material to slip through my fingers. "I am rocking total bed head while you look like you just finished a photo shoot."

He moved an errant strand of hair from my forehead with his fingers gently. "I assure you that you are the most beautiful creature in the world to me. There is nothing I value more. But I will inform my personal tailor you appreciate his effort in making me presentable."

I almost laughed at his use of the word presentable. Humans

walked into things because they were busy staring at Rene when he was in public. But his words to describe me sunk in and I smiled at him. "I still don't know why you are so nice to me."

"Yes, you do; you just aren't ready to accept it. But I do not believe anyone has ever described me as... nice."

"Well, they haven't gotten to know you well enough then."

He stared at me for some time. "Most people are more interested in my power than in... getting to know me."

"I suppose that is accurate of many successful people. Regardless of species."

"I imagine that's true. Are you ready to head to the coven building? It is late in the afternoon and by the time you're ready, dusk will be upon us."

"Sounds good." I got up and ready quickly, and we were heading down the stairs in half an hour.

Cassara was in the foyer speaking to Val when we descended the steps, and she winked at me as we approached. While she always wore a similar leather outfit, this one was actual pants with a leather tank top. "Hey chickee."

"How do you get sexier every time I see you?" I asked.

"It's a gift. You thinking of swinging for the other team?"

I choked. "No, but thanks for the offer."

She laughed and headed for the door. "There is still a bit of sunlight, so stick to the canopy. It's going to prickle a bit until we get in the limo."

The door to the vehicle was already open, and the doorman stood with an umbrella over the back seat entrance. I nodded at him politely as I slid into the car, but Cass was right. My skin felt like I had a slight sunburn until she and Rene joined me, and the door slammed shut.

Cass and I chatted about training and how apologetic Kirnen was after he accidentally sliced me with his blade. The ride was so quick I was disappointed when the vehicle came to a stop and the coven building loomed outside.

"I will wait out here unless you need me, Rene?"

He nodded his head. "I would prefer you stand guard. We can handle Ursula. If any errant mercenaries show up, we all leave immediately."

We exited the vehicle and Rene held the umbrella over me as we walked to the entrance. Ursula surprised me by opening the door herself and backing away to let us enter.

We followed her to the table, and I had barely sat down before Rene spoke.

"We promised to keep you apprised of progress. We found another page of the prophecy. Once we fit some of the pages together, a passage was revealed."

Ursula leaned forward with an eager look on her withered face. It was the first time I had seen her without her full makeup and her black robe had a small stain. It was as if the strain of leadership was getting to her for the first time in her life. "What did it say?"

Rene explained the passage and the effect it had on me. "It was written by the high priestess of that era. Your kind seeks to destroy mine."

Ursula sucked in a breath. "That is not true. We may seek your destruction Rene, but no witch would want the burden of genocide."

I felt the familiar feel of the magical probe and a protection spell formed between Ursula and me. "Stop it. You are not testing my magic anymore and if you seek to assess Rene, you can fucking well ask him if he minds." I rarely swore, but how dare she try to probe Rene or me without consent?

Ursula tried to pierce my bubble with a sharp spike, but it glanced off and the sting of that failed attempt creased her brow. I had botched a spell enough times to know what felt like a slap in the face. "How dare you," she hissed.

"Back at you."

Brigid entered from the side door and paused when she saw Rene and me sitting at the table. It was obvious that Ursula had not informed her second-in-command that we were having a meeting. Her eyes turned from shock to complete outrage and her hands raised in the air before lightning arced from her fingers toward Rene.

I redirected my shield toward her and stood up so I could fight the attack on both fronts. "You bitch."

Ursula stood at the same time I did. While she had attempted to assess Rene, her magic was not intended to harm him. "Brigid. What are you doing? Stop this at once."

Brigid hissed at the high priestess. "You stupid old goat. I tried to lead you to the path of redemption, but you are determined to lead the coven to its destruction. You can die along with the vamp tramp witch and the mad overseer."

Rene stood and stared at Brigid as her electrical storm bounced off my shield. "You were undermining the coven and Ursula's position. You are the witch leading the dark faction."

Brigid hissed under the weight of her power as it flowed from her, usurping her energy. "You are doomed overseer, along with the unholy creatures you call clan."

I felt Ursula strengthen my magical shield, and I assumed that Brigid had no way to hurt us. But the second witch was far craftier than I expected and she grabbed at something from the pocket of her black robe before blowing it into the air. Sparkles glittered around us and I assumed the protection spell would block it.

There was a lesson in every mistake, and I should have known that non-magical dust particles could penetrate a magical shield.

They flitted through like fairy wings and Rene hissed when they landed on his skin.

Flecks of gray marred his cheek as he attempted to wipe the offensive powder from his face.

Ursula stared at Rene's face in horror before turning to Brigid. "You have been murdering the vampires. How could you betray your coven in this way?"

Brigid huffed. "You were so bloated with your power you did not see what was happening right in front of you. I care nothing for this coven and will form my own. We will replace the false human leader and rid the diseased undead from the world."

Ursula hissed. "How dare you speak to me so? I trained you. Gave you every opportunity to be the next high priestess."

Brigid laughed and there was a twinkle of madness as the sound echoed around us. "The fact that you think so is proof of your idiocy. The overseer has been infected and the next stage of our evolution is at hand. It will not include the undead or you." Smoke rose from the floor as misty fingers wrapped around her body. The shroud I had seen on multiple occasions cocooned her before she seemed to vanish before our eyes.

My protection shield died off as I turned to Rene. His hand had several splotches of gray and he appeared to be in the process of turning to stone. "How do I stop it?"

Cass burst through the front door and her jaw dropped when she saw Rene's skin.

Rene held his hand up, and it made a grating sound as he clenched his fingers into a fist. "Strange. It does not hurt. But my body is shutting down." There was a hint of sadness, but none of the hysteria I would have had if I had been poisoned and knew I would die.

Ursula stepped toward Rene with betrayal in her eyes. "Allow me to try to help you."

Rene nodded, and she touched his skin lightly. I had no idea what spell she used, but I felt the power emanating from her, and she was expending a lot of it.

She swayed slightly when she opened her eyes and several wrinkles formed around her mouth. "I have halted the progression of the compound, but it is not a cure. You must find one soon."

Cassara's eye flickered red as her fangs lengthened. "Who did this?"

"Brigid. She is the witch behind the dark faction. We had it wrong, and Rene paid the price."

Ursula dropped her hand and stared at Cassara. "If he dies, it is war. The humans will side with the vampires under these circumstances. Brigid broke the conclave, and every witch will pay the price for her treachery." I wanted to mention that Ursula was okay with killing me at one time, but I was technically a witch then and a member of the coven, so she had some claim to me then.

Cassara's chest heaved. "Where is she, Ursula? I want her location and just so we are clear, you are giving me autonomy to kill her."

Ursula nodded sadly, but the pain in her eyes was real. Brigid had been like a daughter to her. "I don't know where she is. I doubt she will return to her residence, but her shroud is almost impenetrable. Brigid's actions warrant a death sentence. She and any who follow her are no longer under coven protection. I will inform William of this development and we will all work on a cure for Rene. She has no concept of what she has done."

Rene touched my shoulder gently. "Let's return to the mansion. We need to regroup."

Cass pointed at Ursula. "If you helped Brigid in any way, you are dead."

I shook my head. "She didn't Cass. Brigid told her she plans to kill her, too. The dark faction has declared war on basically everybody. I have no idea what they think they can gain under the circumstances."

Cass moved to the door and opened it. "Let's go."

CHAPTER 8

My heart beat an uneven staccato as I tried to calm my raging emotions. Cass and I glanced nervously at one another as Rene settled into the back seat of the limo and she closed the door. The vehicle jerked forward, and our tires spit gravel behind us as the tension in the air pressed down on my chest like a vise. The soft glow of the moon cast an eerie shadow on his mottled cheek, making his pale skin appear even more ethereal. But tonight, it wasn't his otherworldly beauty that held my attention; it was the devastating transformation unfolding before me.

As the limo rallied through the coven forest, my eyes remained glued on his skin. The effects of the vicious compound that was turning his body to stone were painfully apparent. Ursula had slowed the process, but it continued to spread like a smoldering fire consuming its power source. His perfect, handsome features were now frozen in a partial state of paralysis. The cold, gray surface of his skin looked like it had been carved from marble, each feature permanently etched in place.

Icy fingers squeezed my heart, and my breath caught in my throat. The vampire overseer, the man who ignited a fire within me that I had given up on, was fading before my eyes. The pain hit me like a freight train, and I could feel the tears welling in my eyes.

I reached out with a trembling hand before my fingers brushed against his rigid cheek. The unyielding, smooth surface sent a shiver down my spine and panic surged within me. A meltdown would not help Rene, and I took a stuttered breath to calm myself. For all my new magic, my inexperience left Rene vulnerable, and the guilt crashed over me like a tidal wave.

In that agonizing moment, I realized the depth of my feelings. He wasn't just a powerful vampire, or a creature of the night. While I wasn't ready to admit to those feelings, they were very real, and I couldn't imagine being in any clan without him. The devastation on Cassara's face informed me she felt the same. My world was slipping away and taking him with it.

As the limo bounced down the dirt road, every second felt like an eternity. I squeezed Rene's hand, desperate to retain our connection. "Don't leave us, Rene."

He stared at me with a mixture of regret and wonder. "I will be able to withstand the infection for a couple of days. I have slowed blood flow to my body and am in the process of redirecting the damaged tissue to non-imperative organs."

Cass hissed. "This is a cluster fuck of epic proportions. I failed you and I promise that if you die and we go to war, that I will take a thousand of those bitches down before they get me."

My hand trembled over Rene's. There was a reason that everyone feared Cassara. She had given me her trust and friendship and I had enjoyed her fun sense of humor, but this was the vengeful killer that the rest of the world saw. The monster that slipped from the shadows to relinquish those who preyed on the innocent of their lives. "He isn't going to die. We will find the antidote."

Cass huffed. "There is no way to hide this from the clan, Raven."

"We don't need to. In fact, we should enlist their help."

Cass shook her head. "You don't understand. I wish our world was like that, but it isn't."

I stared at her tortured face and huddled close to Rene until we reached the mansion. We exited quietly and there was an audible gasp from the older vampire standing by the door when we entered.

The chatter in the foyer ceased instantly, and every vampire in the large room stared in shock at Rene. While he had been able to halt the progression of the stone patches on his face, his hands were gray and his fingers appeared to be carved from stone.

Val approached Cassara with a face like a thundercloud. "What the fuck happened? How is this possible?"

Cass blinked slowly. "Brigid attacked while I was outside. She used her shroud to get past me or she was already inside, but she used the compound on Rene. If he dies, it's open season on the witches, but Ursula has a death order on Brigid and has excommunicated her from the coven. If anyone gets any information on her location, you tell me immediately." She had raised her voice so every vampire in the room heard her, though she hadn't needed to with their extra-sensory hearing; she was emphasizing her anger, and nobody moved until Dimitri, threaded his way through the crowd with a look of disbelief, when he saw Rene.

"How is he alive? Can he fight the compound killing him?" He spoke to Cassara as if Rene were no longer able to speak for himself.

Cassara's lips pursed. "He is fighting it, and we will look for the antidote. Ursula inferred there was one. She attempted to halt the progression of the disease."

Dimitri's eyes sparkled, and his shock turned to interest. "We must call a clan summit immediately, before he dies."

Rene moved so fast, my hair blew into my face. He held Dmitri by the throat with his arm extended. "In my weakest hour, you are no match for me, Dimitri. Any other vampire would be dead minutes after exposure. You should be more interested in finding a cure so the witches don't exterminate our entire species than concerning yourself with the next overseer. I guarantee you there are far more appropriate contenders from the other clans than you."

The other death dealers ran into the room with their weapons drawn. They extended their spears and aimed them at Dimitri. Cass stepped in front of them and stared at the suspended clan leader. "Until Rene dies, he is in charge. If you issue another order like that, I will stake you and bathe in your blood."

Dimitri held Rene's wrists as his feet dangled in the air. "I apologize for my outburst. I fear for the clans and if you fall, then we will be in complete disarray. The witches will annihilate us without an overseer. Our unity is what makes us strong. No single clan could withstand this kind of war."

Rene lowered him slowly to the ground. "That is true Dimitri, but I put contingencies in place for my death centuries ago."

Dimitri coughed when Rene released his neck. "What contingencies?"

Rene rolled his shoulders, and the sound of stone grating against itself echoed around us. "You will find out when I leave this world, but I assure you that you won't like it."

Dimitri's eyes widened, and his face held a mixture of fear and surprise. "It won't happen again. I apologize. Your... condition is concerning."

Cass motioned to the stairs. "Rene, let's get you up to your suite."

Rene grabbed my hand and turned toward the stairs. While his face remained impassive, his anger rolled off him in waves. Dimitri had waited more than ten seconds before basically declaring Rene unfit to rule all the clans. Two thousand years of knowledge and power were worthless to the Shadow Bone leader. As if he believed he was better equipped to withstand a supernatural war. How inflated could one ego be?

Cass darted ahead of us and opened the door to the suite, holding it until Rene and I were safely inside. Val and Quinn entered before she closed the door and the three leather-clad death dealers stood like sentries, regarding their leader.

Rene released my hand and sat down on the bed. He held up one hand and turned up his palm. Every finger was completely gray and looked like a perfect statue. "Cass, I need you and the death dealers to look for Brigid. I do not require guards in my personal suite."

Cass pointed at the door. "Did you see what happened down there? Dimitri is like a fucking vulture. He's practically drooling at the opportunity to replace you. If he calls for a vote of no confidence, we are all doomed."

Rene smiled, but a part of his face didn't react like it should. "Trust me, Cassara. This is not the first time a clan head has attempted to overthrow me. It has simply been some time since it happened. Even if I am confined to a bed, the clan is about to realize the true extent of my power and the fate that awaits them if I die."

Cass looked less sure of herself. "That sounds bad."

Rene shrugged. "It would be more challenging for you than most, but for much different reasons."

Cassara looked like she wanted to ask more, but Rene's eyelids drooped. "Get some rest. I will do as you ask, but one death dealer will remain in the mansion at all times. You call if you need him."

"Agreed," Rene said.

Cass opened the door and Val and Quinn filed out before she exited and closed it. I moved to sit on the bed beside Rene, and pulled me beside him. I was nestled against his body and despite the grisly transformation, he felt warm to my touch.

His fingers traced my back, and I was glad I couldn't see them. "I have imagined my death many times, but never like this. The irony of turning to stone when I have lived hundreds of years feeling as if my heart was just as cold as any statue is not lost on me."

I place my hand on his heart. "You aren't cold, Rene, and you aren't going to die. I will do everything in my power to ensure you beat this thing."

He stared at the ceiling for some time. "There is only one way to boost my power. You are not ready for it."

I leaned up on one arm. "You know a way to reverse the effects of this compound?"

"Yes. Without an antidote, the only way to counteract this poison is for me to bond with you. Even though you are a vampire, you were exposed, and your power made you immune to its effects."

I couldn't deny what he was saying. I felt the sparkly dust touch my skin, but there was no reaction. "Is there any other way?" With all the surrounding betrayal, I wouldn't lie to him. He was right. I wasn't ready to commit to anyone let alone the most powerful creature on earth.

"Not that I am aware of. Ursula seemed to think there was an antidote, but she didn't know what it was. I am pretty sure she is looking as we speak. She understands the consequences of my death better than the Shadow Bone clan."

I pursed my lips. "Dimitri mentioned something to me about bonding. May I ask you some questions?"

"Raven, you never need permission to ask me anything. No matter how difficult the subject, I will tell you the truth."

"Dimitri said that if you bond with a member of Shadow Bone you are required to take a wife from each of the other clans. Is that true?"

His eyes flickered red. "It is, but I've already taken steps to rectify that issue. Certain concessions were put in motion the moment I met you. All I can ask is that you trust me."

"I do, but I need time to think about the bonding thing. Nobody should be forced into a decision of that magnitude, but I guarantee we will find an antidote. I have an idea. In this, I need you to trust me."

Rene turned his head to meet my gaze. "I do."

"Good. Tell me about the bonding ceremony. Is it like a wedding?"

He smiled slightly. "In some ways. It is performed on a full moon by a specific priest, if you will. But the attendees are those the bonding couple hold dear. It is a distinct honor to be invited to such an event."

I smiled. "I bet you have been invited to a lot of them over the years."

"Admittedly, as overseer, I have witnessed the ceremony on many occasions. There was little joy for me, knowing I would never have what they did. You changed everything. If this is the end of my life, then I want you to allow Cass to help you. Learn the beauty our world has to offer and enjoy it to the best of your ability. You are a gift to not only this clan, but our entire species."

I touched his face, and my fingers trailed to his chin. "Don't talk like that. You are not going anywhere. You promised to trust me."

"With my life," he whispered.

I leaned down so our lips touched. The kiss was slow, and my heart leaped with emotions I was not ready to explore. He was everything I ever wanted, and I was losing him. My hand slipped to his hair, and I clutched the silky strands as if I could hold him to me forever. When I finally released him, his gaze met mine with the same fire and passion he always had when in my arms.

"Consider my proposal. I want you no matter the circumstances. Whether it is for a day or a century. But I don't want you to think I want to bond with you because I was infected with the compound. I have been leading you toward this from the moment I walked into the human morgue. I love you."

CHAPTER 9

*L*ying there in our opulent but dimly-lit room, the weight of his words hung in the air like a brittle promise. I believed every word, and the response caught in my throat. Rene's confession was wrenched from his soul like a bittersweet melody that mingled with the reality of our situation. The grisly compound continued to slowly suck out the undead life within him. His vibrant skin was stilled, mottled with patches of gray that increased in size with every passing second. His once-vibrant eyes were now clouded with doubt, and while he said there was no pain, I wasn't sure I believed him. His gaze held mine with an intensity that sent shivers down my spine. As if he wanted my face to be the last thing he saw when he left this life.

It was an outcome I would never be able to live with despite his plea for me to carry on. I shifted closer to him, feeling the gentle warmth of his body against mine, yet unable to escape the cold reality that threatened to rip us apart. The tenderness of his words was in complete opposition to the harsh truth of his condition, a cruel reminder that immortality was an illusion, even for a vampire as powerful as Rene.

His voice held a weakness it hadn't before, as if he accepted his death. His plea possessed a sincerity that had pierced the darkness of the situation and wrapped my soul in love and light. His confession of love was monumental on so many levels and I was frozen in place as I stared at his still, handsome features. And in that moment, the world seemed to pause, as if Mother Nature herself was holding her breath, waiting for me to respond.

My heart swelled, and emotions I thought I left in the past welled up within me like a tidal wave. I reached out and gently brushed a strand of hair away from his forehead, and my fingers traced the contours of his face with a mixture of affection and desperation. The truth in his eyes was undeniable, and it echoed the feelings I had harbored deep within my own heart. The ones I wasn't ready to admit to, especially now. When his death was imminent if I was unsuccessful in my quest to save him.

Red tears formed on my lashes, threatening to overflow, as I struggled to find the words to convey the depth of my emotions. Honesty was the only defense in the face of adversity. In the face of his impending death, the vulnerability of the moment hit me like a lightning rod. "I love you too," I whispered with my voice echoing a raw honesty that matched his own.

His lips curved into a smile that could stop time. There was a mix of relief and contentment in his expression, as if he had waited an eternity for this moment. One last triumph before he took his final rest. My soul clung to him in the midst of the uncertainty and reverence, and I found solace in the connection we had forged amidst the chaos of strife. The odds had been against us, and we had overcome adversity and prejudice. Now we just needed to conquer death itself. No small feat for any being, whether supernatural or human.

As I clung to him, his heart began to beat a steady rhythm against my palm. As if his soul wanted me to know that this love was more real than any power he possessed. A single light in the midst of eternal darkness. It was a force that defied every obstacle put in its path. A flame that burned brighter no matter the shadows that surrounded it. And even as the cruel compound continued its vicious work of robbing Rene of his life force, I found strength in his admission. His love was forever, whether that was a moment, a day, or forever. I knew that no matter what happened in the coming days, we were united in this eternal war and nothing could break our conviction.

Rene touched my cheek. "Be with me. Tonight, while I still have the strength to give you the pleasure you deserve."

My heart stuttered. "It might hurt you."

Rene's smile was like a cat that had caught a mouse. "You couldn't hurt me. Your presence brings me nothing but pleasure."

I loved his response, and my entire body vibrated. I felt his arousal against my leg, and excitement soared through me. I sat up and removed my clothes, but when he attempted to do the same, I placed my palm on his chest. "Allow me."

His eyes flickered with red as I slowly removed his clothes. In truth, I went far slower than necessary, attempting to draw out the moment. This could be our last time together, and I wanted it to be special. To show him how much his faith in me meant. The truth of my words.

After I deposited his clothes on the floor next to mine, my hand traced the defined muscles of his chest, avoiding the patches of gray before I wrapped my fingers around his cock. The feel of him in my hand was empowering and made me feel sexier than ever. He was all hard flesh surrounded by silky skin and I moved up and down his long length, making him groan.

"Life held no meaning for me before you. It was an endless set of tasks I performed out of duty. There is nothing more beautiful than you touching me." His deep voice stroked me like a caress.

Rene had given me everything since the first time he saw me. I hadn't realized the burdens of being the overseer or the isolation it inevitably created. I ran a finger over the flared tip, and moisture leaked onto my hand before I continued to stroke him.

I stopped what I was doing and stared into his loving eyes. He was fully engaged with what I was doing, as if he couldn't wait to see what I would do next. "I love you and I'm not saying it because you were exposed to the compound. I have felt this way for a while, but it's hard for me to... trust people. I haven't exactly had stellar luck in the love department."

"There is no measurement for what I feel for you, but we are going to leave Isra out of this. I cannot imagine another male touching you. And I struggle to control myself, even though I know neither of you would pursue a relationship again." His words were punctuated with a growl that sent a shiver down my spine. But it wasn't fear; it was arousal. His possessiveness in this one aspect made me feel cherished.

"Isra is my best friend and always will be, but he wasn't who I was talking about. Isra is more attracted to you than to me." I kissed his abdomen. "Perhaps I should be worried. He is awfully attractive." I felt his muscles tense beneath my lips, and I could sense him smile.

"You are teasing me. Even now, you bring light to the darkness. I need you, Raven. In a way, that will take eons for you to understand."

I wanted to respond, but Rene flipped me onto my back so quickly, my breath caught in my lungs. He was on top of me, with his arousal pressing against my core.

My eyes slipped closed as he slid his erection through my slick folds. "I need you too." It was true, and the admission sprung from my soul like a geyser.

Rene propped himself up before he slid the blunt tip over my aching core, sending my desire skyrocketing. I was surprised at how quickly my insides melted and the coil tightened in my abdomen, searching for release. That ultimate high that only my vampire lover could gift me.

His mouth returned to mine as his lips teased me. As I was getting caught up in his kiss, and time seemed to melt away, he pushed the swollen head into my tight channel. I cried out as my body tightened around him and the pressure increased. The euphoria of having him inside me was like being in another stratosphere and I clutched his shoulders, praying this was the start of a long life together and not the end.

"Relax, little bird. I seek only your pleasure. Forget the events of this evening and allow yourself to soar with me." His mouth moved to my breast then and flicked a nipple. The sensation sent a wave of pleasure through me, and my muscles relaxed. I hadn't realized I was so tense until he mentioned it, but it felt like a belt loosening.

Rene slipped his hand between our bodies and rubbed my sensitive nub. Sweat dripped from his forehead as he remained in place, concentrating on the slow rhythm he created. He never complained about the restraint it took to ensure I experienced the ultimate pleasure when we were together. His patience was as impressive as his manhood and his power. As he stroked me, my hips automatically responded, and I moved against his hand.

"Fly with me, little bird. Prove that those years of loneliness were worth every tortuous second." His voice was low and deep, but I was too caught up in what he was doing to respond, so I nodded and kissed his lips. His finger never stopped thrumming my nub while he moved slowly in and out of me.

"That feels so damn good. Don't stop." The confession was ripped from my soul like a talisman.

He smiled at me as he pulled out and thrust back in. I arched toward him, allowing more access as his thumb continued to press my nub, and his mouth nibbled my neck. He gradually increased the tempo, then gazed into my eyes, showing me how much he loved me. There was no denying that look. It was strife, hope, and resilience. All wrapped in a handsome dark bow of power. A gift to me alone. And I thanked god for it as he continued the sensual slide into my body.

His thick shaft was an iron rod pistoning in and out of me as he increased his speed. My desire took over, and in seconds, I was moving with him. Matching each thrust with my own. The coil in my abdomen began to tighten as I reached the breaking point of my arousal.

Rene's fingers twinned with mine before he brought them over my head. His thrusts intensified, leaving me powerless to do anything but bask in the erotic fire he created. "Let me taste you. Draw your blood." He had promised me he would never take my blood without permission, but I would have given him anything at that moment.

"Yes."

He groaned against my neck a second before his fangs punctured the flesh where my shoulder met my neck. The sensation was an intoxicating blend of pain and pleasure. The initial sting was sharp, a quick, almost electric jolt that made me gasp. But as his teeth sank deeper, the pain began to ebb, replaced by a warm, pulsing sensation that radiated through my body.

My heartbeat quickened, each thud echoing in my ears, syncing with the rhythmic pull of his feeding. The world around me seemed to blur, the edges softening as I focused on the connection between us. There was an intimacy in the act, a merging of our essences that went beyond the physical.

A slow, tingling warmth spread from the bite, coursing through my veins like liquid fire. It was both soothing and exhilarating, a heady mix that made me feel alive in a way nothing else could. The bond between us deepened with each moment, a silent communication that spoke of trust, need, and an unbreakable connection.

I could feel Rene's strength, his presence enveloping me, grounding me in the here and now. His hands cradled my shoulders, steadying me as he drank, his touch a gentle anchor amidst the storm of sensations. I leaned into him, my own need mirroring his, our breaths mingling in the stillness.

As he withdrew the sharp burn of his teeth sent me hurtling over the edge and my orgasm washed over me like a marauding tsunami. His momentum increased before he joined me in blissful oblivion.

Coming together as one was the greatest high of my life, and I never wanted it to end. I cursed Brigid for trying to take Rene from the world. His power and intelligence were nothing compared to the compassion he let few see. I sighed contently as he moved his hips, and mini orgasms trickled through my body. Nobody could compare to Rene. If I lost him, there would be no other.

He moved to lie beside me and pulled me onto his shoulder.

My fingers traced his chest. "Do you only bite during sex?"

Rene kissed my forehead. "I will bite you often, but only to bring you pleasure. That is, of course, if you enjoyed it."

"You know I did."

"I hope in time you will return the experience. That is if..."

I placed my finger on his lips. "Don't say it. You are stuck here... with me. Got it?"

Rene met my gaze. "Whatever my lady desires."

CHAPTER 10

I hadn't meant to drift off. But I woke in the dimly-lit room, with the remnants of a nightmare swirling at the edge of my subconscious. The memory of Brigid's attack was burned into my mind, an unsettling mix of fear and despair that sent shivers down my spine. Meanwhile, the crumpled sheets whispered of the passion we had shared, and I tried not to think it was the last time.

My face turned to the figure beside me, and I took in Rene's serene presence. The vampire whose touch ignited a pleasure I had never known and left me wanting more. His once-smooth and perfect skin now held a gray roughness that denoted the poison slowly spreading through his veins. Half of his once-beautiful complexion had turned to a pitted granite. A cruel reminder we were running out of time. I had to consider bonding with him soon, but Rene had warned me there were no guarantees. Even a link to me may not save him.

I reached out tentatively, and my fingers traced the jawline of his ashen skin. The contrast between the sandpaper feel of stone and the remaining softness was a harsh reminder of the fallacy of immortality. His eyes were closed, and he took shallow breaths, which alerted me he was fighting an internal battle. That subtle rise and fall was a rhythmic reminder that life still coursed through his veins, while tainted by the compound that threatened to destroy him.

The moonlight filtered through the curtains, casting a subtle glow over his ashen features. The pain in my chest was like a stake in the heart, a sharp reminder that time was slipping through our fingers like grains of sand. Amidst the turmoil of my emotions, I recalled his declaration of love and accepted the undeniable beauty of the moment. Ours was a fierce love that refused to be extinguished.

As I watched him rest, the weight of our predicament pressed down on me like a knee on my chest. The attack, our unrequited passion, and the whispers of love in the night wove a tapestry of emotions that I couldn't escape. I knew that the poison was killing him. Despite his age and power, he had become as fragile as the rest of us. A victim of hate and jealousy.

But as the reality of our situation threatened to overwhelm me, I found solace in him next to me. The sensation of his roughened skin beneath my fingertips was a reminder that love was a reward and every couple had to work to retain it. For us to endure it, we would have to weather the harshest of storms. And as I leaned in to press a soft kiss against his cheek, I vowed to fight for him and hold on to the moments we had. I would use every ounce of power I possessed to save him and cherish the time we had left, no matter how fleeting it was.

"Good morning, little bird," Rene whispered before his eyes opened.

I smiled and met his bloodshot eyes. "Hey. How are you feeling?"

"I wish to ease your fears, but I am afraid my time is coming to an end," he said.

"When is the next full moon? When can we bond?"

His eyes held a sadness that ripped my heart from my chest and stomped it beneath my boot. "It is in two days. I am sorry, Raven. I will not make it. But I want you to know how much it means to me you would have accepted me."

"No!" I hissed.

His smile was slight as he fought to utilize the muscles in his face. But my response was interrupted by a scream from downstairs. I rushed from the bed and dashed to the closet. I had my leather pants, a white T-shirt, and a black jacket on in record time before zipping my boots.

Cass burst through the door as I exited the closet, and I found her staring at Rene's exposed chest. He hadn't moved from the bed as Cass and I shared a painful glance.

"Rene?" Cass whispered.

"What has happened?" he croaked.

"Brigid is downstairs demanding that we turn over Raven. She is threatening to expose the entire foyer. There are over a hundred clan members in the room. And she has backup. There are a dozen mercenaries with her."

Rene attempted to get up but fell back against the covers. "I cannot help you with this. I am sorry."

Cassara's chest heaved. "You are dying. You are actually going to leave us on the brink of a war."

Rene stared at Cassara. "I would never have left you by choice. You have been my lone confidant until Raven. I would never have waited for her if not for you."

I grabbed Cassara's arm. "He is not dying. Take me to Brigid, but station someone in here you trust. I don't want him alone."

"Val is outside. He will remain at the door until we return."

I pointed at Rene. "Don't move or I swear you will regret it."

Rene's lip twitched. "You are fortunate I am physically unable to."

Cass opened the door, and we jogged to the end of the hallway after nodding to Val. She stopped me at the top of the stairs, knowing the danger that lurked in the foyer. "What do you want to do?"

"I need you to stay up here. Watch but don't interfere. If she unleashes that compound, everyone in that room dies, including you. Rene has only this long because he is ancient, but the rest of you will be dust before I can force her to give me an antidote."

Cassara's eyes flickered. "You honestly think she is going to give you a cure?"

I grunted. "Not by asking nicely."

Cass smiled. "That's why I like you so much."

I touched her arm. "This could get... bad. I am immune to the compound, but I am not sure Brigid knows that. She left before we saw the effects it had on Rene."

"She may also think your shield protected you."

"True. Either way, this will not go smoothly and there are likely to be casualties."

Cass flinched. "I understand. Saving Rene is the priority."

"Agreed." I stepped from the hallway to the top landing and glanced down at Brigid as I descended the stairs. I went deliberately slow, so I could ascertain the location of the mercenaries and the clan members they held hostage with black velvet pouches in their hands.

The clan members huddled near the walls, attempting to make themselves smaller, but a single speck of the dust in those tiny satchels was a death sentence to every person in the room. Except me and the dark faction holding them hostage.

I reached the bottom stair and the mercenaries closest to me moved to allow me within the circle they had created around Brigid. She looked like a black-robed princess among her dark knights and her sneer alerted me she was enjoying being the center of attention. Ursula hadn't noticed the envy of her second-in-command or her need to be in control. She would

FORTY DEATHS TILL US PART

bring this entire world to the brink of destruction with her bid for power.

"Brigid, if you wanted to chat, you simply could have called."

Brigid smiled. "I can't infect you over the phone."

Part of me was happy she thought she could kill me, but that meant she was going to kill everyone else in the room when she unleashed her deadly retribution. "Why do this Brigid? You would have been the high priestess soon. Ursula is getting up there in age."

"The old bag would never have retired. I would have been in my sixties before the mantle was passed."

"So you are starting a war because you are impatient."

One of the mercenaries turned. "Shut up Blood Witch. We are only here for you. Nobody else needs to die."

I arched an eyebrow. "She already attacked the overseer. He was infected by the compound. When he dies, it's war. Surely you know this."

Several men glanced at one another. "She lies. Brigid didn't attack Rene."

I realized Brigid had manipulated the ex-PSO members. They hated the vampires. That was obvious, but they hadn't signed up for an all-out war. "Do you want to tell them, or should I?"

"There is nothing to say." Brigid raised her arms in the air with a malevolent smile.

My power rose within me, flaring outward like an iridescent bubble. It encased Brigid and the mercenaries, forming a glittering barrier between the clan members and the lethal powder in their hands. This protection was not limited to magic and while it looked like anyone could step through it, that was the illusion. Fortunately, Brigid was more interested in hurting me than worrying about the kind of ward I placed over us. She hurtled a flaming ball of fire, which I countered with one of my own. The two powerful forces collided in the air as sparks burst around us in a shower of embers. The air crackled with an electrifying energy as our magics sought dominance over the other. I was a witch on a mission and if I failed, Rene would die. I stood unwavering, as I tried to come up with a way to force Brigid's compliance. Magic was the obvious choice, but she seemed as powerful as me. She stood with tendrils of her shroud warping around her robes, though she remained visible. Still, her presence cast an ominous shadow over the foyer and those who watched within it.

The clan seemed to hold its breath, as she sent energy balls and black shadows to rob me of my life. While I was new to this level of power, my instincts had been honed over the years of harnessing the purest energies. They guided me through the barrage of spells and incantations. When she sent a web of dark matter hurtling toward me. Tendrils of light swirled around me, forming an intricate web of protection, while Brigid hissed in anger.

With each flick of our wrists and each whispered word, our magic surged forth in a breathtaking display of power and will. My spells were of the light, and seeking protection. They wove intricate patterns of radiant energy that accented the beauty of the foyer. But her magic was a tempest of shadows, fueled by hate that sought our destruction. It seethed with malice and crackled with dark intent.

As our magic clashed, the air grew thick with tension and smoke filled the protection bubble, obscuring our view of the room. The floor beneath us trembled as another energy blast collided in midair and the castoff cracked the opulent tile. But Brigid was unrelenting, and her spells were fueled by a tenacious hunger for dominion and death. Her shroud of shadows stretched and twisted, forming nightmarish specters that threatened to break.

As the battle raged on, the floor bore the scars of our conflict.

Black patches of tar and gouges in the once-pristine tile created an apocalyptic effect as the mercenaries all ducked, attempting to avoid the surrounding chaos. They had been trapped inside my protection and many were regretting their decision to help the mad witch battling me. In the depths of our struggle, I noticed a decline in the strength of Brigid's power. Her expenditure of magic had exacted its toll. Mine was waning as well, and I prayed for a miracle if my protection shield fell.

"Raven, constrain Brigid, so I may speak with her." Rene's voice echoed around me, even though I couldn't see him. Why hadn't I considered his natural abilities?

With a final burst of determination, I channeled the force within me, and a radiant whip of light pierced through the shadows. The air shimmered with a blinding brilliance, ropes of light wrapped around Brigid's torso. She screamed as her power began to wane and her spells faltered. With a triumphant exhale, the surrounding shroud receded, leaving her like a lassoed animal for all to see.

I turned to the mercenaries huddled at the edges of my protection spell. "Drop the pouches or you will be tied up like a roped steer."

The mercenaries dropped the lethal compound, and I retracted my spell. The bubble dropped to reveal an empty room, except for Rene and his death dealers. He had used my protection to send the clan members to safety, but he looked worse than ever and both Quinn and Val were forced to help him stand. They had dressed him in simple black pants and a T-shirt, but his arms were completely gray as was most of his face.

"Can you get the antidote?" I asked.

Brigid continued to struggle with her lasso made of light as Rene approached her. "I can invade her thoughts. It was kind of her to deliver her mind to me."

"No!" she hissed as Cassara extended her staff and her spear glinted against the overhead light of the chandelier. Val and Quinn helped him to the center of the room, where he placed his granite-like fingers against her temple.

Rene was quiet as he scanned her memories. "I have it. When I am stronger, I will have another... chat with her. I am too weak to press her further without killing her."

Brigid spit on his shirt, then turned to me. "Raven helped create the compound that is killing you overseer. She may make an antidote, but she won't be able to make it in time to save you."

"I never helped create anything like that," I snapped.

Brigid sneered at me. "But you did. Star Canyon is the main ingredient. You grew it so beautifully, but now you are a monster, and you no longer have access to the seeds."

"We will see about that. Rene, text me the ingredients. Cass, will you be coming with me to Powerful Petals, or do you need to stay here and stake Brigid?"

Cass stared at Brigid with open hatred. "Val will kill her if she so much as breathes wrong."

William entered the front door with two teams of PSO officers. They apprehended the mercenaries, and in under a minute, they were walking back to the front door. I turned away from Brigid to watch them leave. The momentary distraction cost me, and a stabbing pain pierced my skull before the shroud wrapped around Brigid and she disappeared.

Cass bolted toward the dark witch's location, but when her spear swung through the air, it was empty. "Where is she?"

I grabbed my skull. "She pierced my protection. It's like an ice pick in the brain, but she used most of her magic. She needs time to recuperate. We will worry about her later. We need to get the Star Canyon and Powerful Petals is the only place in town that has all the ingredients."

I shook off the fire in my brain and gave Rene a quick kiss on the cheek before jogging from the building with Cass. We grabbed a small black sports car and were roaring down the road as the PSO officers continued to load the mercenaries into the vans they had driven to clan property in.

The road blurred by as Cass drove at dizzying speed.

"How are you going to get Deanna to give you the ingredients?" she asked.

"I am not asking her. She will be unconscious in ten seconds if she so much as sneezes in my direction. I have had it with the coven."

Cassara's lips pursed. "Good."

She screeched to a stop in front of the store. It was early, but Deanna was already there creating the arrangements. I used magic to unlock the door and stormed in with my power crackling around me.

Deanna rushed from the back room and sucked in a breath when she saw me. "Raven?"

"Don't speak. Just give me the Star Canyon and everything else I need. If you so much as look at me the wrong way, I will burn this building to the ground."

Deanna glanced down. "Ursula said to help you in any way we can. Nobody knew what Brigid was doing. The humans are siding with the vampires. The witches will be destroyed."

"Hatred and idiocy are a deadly combination. Give me the flower."

Deanna rushed to the back and returned with a canister. "I don't have any mature flowers. Brigid took those a few days ago, but here are all the seeds I have."

I took the canister unceremoniously. "I need a few more things, but they aren't rare." I went to the flowers and picked the petals I needed as well as a fern Rene had noted as part of the antidote. The ingredients were benign on their own but had a deadly effect when combined.

"Can you save him?" Deanna asked.

I grunted. Ursula had obviously told the coven what happened to Rene. "Fine time to worry about Rene. He was the only thing keeping the conclave stable. You are all idiots. The coven will be responsible for the deaths of millions if Rene dies."

Deanna looked like she was about to throw up. "I know."

I collected the last of the ingredients. "Let's go, Cass."

CHAPTER 11

*W*e exited the store and got into the SUV as Cass got a text on her phone. "Shit."

"What is it?"

"Dimitri is riling the natives. The clan is losing confidence in Rene. A blind man can see he will be incapacitated soon. Val isn't sure it is safe to treat him at the mansion."

I swore under my breath. "There is a small stove in the store. Let me... ask Deanna to leave, and I will prepare the antidote here. Can you make arrangements to have Rene brought here while I tell Deanna she is lending me the store for an hour? Just come a minute or two after she leaves."

Cass nodded. "That works. Get rid of your ex-partner. I may lose my shit if I confront her."

The interior light flashed on as I opened the door. "I figured."

The door slammed shut before I returned to the store with my supplies. The door chimed as I entered, and Deanna rushed to the front.

"Do you need something else?" she asked.

"Yeah. The store. You will give me an hour alone to make what I need, and I will lock up when I am done."

She looked like she wanted to argue, but her fingers moved to the black apron with the logo for Powerful Petals on the front. "Of course. I am almost done with the arrangements. I can grab a coffee and a bagel before I come back."

There was a small pang of regret as she mentioned the coffee. We had been getting that same breakfast order for over fifteen years. "Good idea."

Deanna put her apron on the counter and left through the front door as I made my way to the back. We used the stove for cooking our own meals, mostly. It was old, but it worked, and I put a silver pot on the burner before placing all the ingredients I would need on the small counter beside it.

I was so engrossed in my work I barely noticed the click of the back door and I didn't look up as a figure joined me in the room. "Are they on their way?"

In the quiet haven of my former flower shop, I continued the delicate dance of blending herbs for an antidote. Every additive gave me a sense of purpose with the goal of saving Rene and preventing a war. The earthy aroma of potted plants and recent blooms centered me and reminded me of the countless hours I had spent in this oasis. With the fragrant promise of healing, my fingers worked deftly to create the life-saving antidote.

I was about to turn and find out why Cass hadn't answered me when an unexpected jolt ripped into my neck. The sharp sting shattered my tranquil resolve as my hand flew to the source of the pain. I blinked as my fingers closed around a tiny, barbed object. I pulled it out, as confusion and shock replaced my bubble of tranquility.

Panic bloomed in my chest as I stumbled back with a wildfire of emotions coursing through me. This pain was unlike anything I had experienced before. It was like a thunderbolt into my bloodstream and my vision wavered before I grabbed the corner of the table we used to create our arrangements at the store. Who did this to me?

My eyes lifted, before my gaze locked onto a man I had never seen before. While he was a stranger, I recognized his black military gear. He had once been a PSO officer, but had agreed to work for Brigid. Obviously, he wasn't part of the attack back at the mansion, but that spiteful witch seemed to have an army at her disposal, and it was clear who her main target was. His aura radiated danger, a stark contrast to the delicate flowers surrounding me. I understood his motives, but I needed to stay alive long enough to help Rene. Cass was coming. I just had to hold on.

The searing pain in my neck was moving through my bloodstream, a pulsating reminder that I had let down my guard. I clenched my fists, willing myself to stay strong in the force of the odds against me.

The antidote I was crafting was all but forgotten, as a fierce resolve took root within me. This man had tried to catch me off guard, but I was no victim. I was powerful, and he was about to understand the consequences of an attack on me.

I raised my hands and called on the well of power coursing through me. Electrified whips of light exploded from my fingers, arcing toward him like tendrils of lightning. He dropped the dart gun and bolted back out the back room door before Cass ran in.

"What happened?" she asked.

I pointed to the dart on the ground. "I think it's Dark Dahlia."

Cass picked up the dart and smelled it. "It is. But there is something else I don't recognize."

I had figured as much, but I hadn't wanted to scare her. Rene was the first priority. He needed to survive. "Is he on his way?"

Cass frowned as she stared at the dart. "Yes. He will be here in a few minutes. Do you need help with the antidote?"

I pointed at the plants on the counter beside the stove. "Put all those in the pot. I want to see if I can purge whatever poison he hit me with."

Cass began to place the petals and leaves I had collected from the shop into the pot as I focused on the fire burning through my blood. I could almost see the dark particles infecting the cells around them and when I realized there was no way to stop the infection, I did the same thing Rene did to stall his death. I slowed my blood flow to the brink of death and my limbs became heavy and my fingertips numb.

It would be difficult to keep my poisoning from Rene for long, but I had to complete the antidote before he found out the truth.

I made my way to the stove as Cass put the last of the ingredients in. "That's good. I am going to do a binding spell to increase potency. This antidote borders on alchemy. The wood chips and various elements go beyond the realm of a mere potion." I touched the handle of the pot and sent a surge of power into the contents. They flickered before returning to a dark brown, warm elixir.

The front door chimed, and Cass sucked in a breath.

"What is it?"

"Constantine," she whispered. There was a whisper of fear, and I knew she feared no man in a fight. Rene's oldest friend scared her on another level, and I turned as he helped Rene into the room.

The overseer was weaker than ever, and Cass helped Constantine place him in the wooden chair in the storeroom.

My gaze moved from Rene's ashen skin to the man helping him get comfortable in the chair.

Constantine's face was stern, as if his anger were barely leashed. His stern angular features held an ageless allure, despite the rugged lines etched into his forehead. The pale-yellow color of his eyes reminded me of a cat and hinted at the countless years he had endured. His chiseled jawline exuded his determination to see Rene returned to his former health, and he dared anyone who opposed his mission with each graceful movement.

He had several weapons clipped to his belt, but my gaze continued to wander back to his eyes.

"Wow," I whispered.

Cass grunted. "Don't gawk. He has an ego the size of Russia as it is."

I held my hand out to him. "I'm Raven. It is a pleasure to meet you. Sorry for... gawking. You have the most unusual eyes I have ever seen. Beautiful though."

Constantine bowed slightly after he pulled his arm from supporting Rene. He shook my hand and glanced at Cassara. "The pleasure is mine, Raven. Do not mind Cassara. She is under the misconception I am here to encroach on her territory."

Cass ran her tongue over an extended fang. "Why are you here?"

Rene crouched. "I asked him to come. There has been a contingency in place for hundreds of years. Constantine and the warriors are it. They will assume control of the clans until a leader they respect is put in power and ensure that none of the clan members go rogue during the reselection process. Their administration is temporary but necessary."

Cass froze. "You will impose military law on the clans?"

Constantine looked her over slowly. "That is the human term for it, yes."

"I'm nobody's bitch, Constantine. Especially yours."

Constantine arched an eyebrow. "I have never sought to be your... boss. The years have made you even more judgmental. I had hoped your time as Rene's personal advisor would soften some of your prejudices."

Cass continued to stir the elixir in the pot as I tramped down the nausea in my stomach. "Is it bubbling yet, Cass?" I asked.

"Just starting to, now."

"Just another minute or two, then. How are you feeling, Rene? Can you push the antidote through your bloodstream? It has to get to all the affected tissue."

Rene nodded, but there were distinct cracks in his ashen skin. "Constantine knows what to do to protect you both. You will stand by his side, Cassara. Promise me."

Cassara's eyes lowered, but I could see the stiffness in her neck as she nodded. "Of course."

I moved to the pot and took over for Cassara. The thickness was like molasses and the exact consistency I needed, so I poured it into a mug from the counter with a picture of a kitten on it.

I passed the mug to Rene. "Drink it while it is warm. It will mix with your blood easier if it doesn't cool."

Rene gulped the liquid down and made a gagging noise. "That is vile."

Cass put her hands on her hips. "Not as vile as death. Don't be such a baby."

Constantine grunted. "You have not changed a bit."

She cocked her head toward him. "Did you honestly think I would?"

Constantine shrugged. "Not really, but I have always enjoyed a challenge."

Rene held up his hand as the rigid limb started to change color. The process wasn't instant, but his true skin color began to emerge in patches, and I assumed the same was happening all over his body.

Constantine stared at the transformation in wonder. "You did it."

I grabbed the edge of the stove when my head began to spin.

Rene stood. "Raven, what is it?"

Cass grabbed the dart from the counter. "She was shot with

this before she made the potion. Brigid has many more acolytes than the ones we already arrested."

Rene took the dart from Cassara and smelled it. "Dark Dahlia, Belladonna, and turmeric. This is witch sickness personified. The Dark Dahlia ensures your vampire metabolism can't fight back."

Cass glanced at me. "Witch sickness? What is that?"

Constantine looked like a thundercloud on steroids, but it was nothing compared to the devastation on Rene's face. The warrior rubbed his chin.

"Vampires were restricted from creating this poison after the accords. It has fallen out of disuse. Few even know this exists or how to make it."

Cass grabbed my arm. "I thought you were going to purge it. Why are you still sick?"

"The combination is a death sentence. She may have been able to purge one of the poisons, but turmeric is a natural blood thinner and reduces the potency of her magic while the poisons kill her."

Cass glanced between the men and me. I knew what she would ask and the answer. "Fix it."

Rene ran his hand through his hair. He was returning to his handsome self by the second. "There is no cure for witch sickness. I cannot believe Brigid would use such a potion. It almost destroyed the coven in ancient times."

Cassara grabbed her chest as if her heart was about to explode. "No. We can't lose her. She is a vampire, too. Why isn't she bouncing back?"

Constantine stared at me. "She is empowered. Vampire or not, she cannot change what she is."

Cass shook her head. "There has to be a way. She found a cure for you. We have to find one for her."

Constantine's eyes flickered. "There is no cure. Her only chance is to bond with Rene and take his blood. This is a choice only she can make. Once he has purged the compound from his blood, and if she agrees, we should prepare. The full moon is tomorrow night. She must stay alive until we can bind them.

Rene stepped up to me, and I allowed him to support my weight. "Bond with me, Raven, do not condemn me to an eternity alone. I beg you to hold on. Just one day of pain and I promise to make every day after, worth it."

CHAPTER 12

*A*s the poison continued its insidious work, spreading through my veins, I could feel its deadly touch, like dark tentacles consuming my vitality. My vibrant energy ebbed like an outgoing tide, leaving me with a heaviness that crushed my spirit and my soul. My body was engaged in an arduous battle, fighting against an unseen enemy, and with every passing moment, brought me closer to eternal darkness.

The power that had surged through me like a tsunami was now a mere trickle, leaving me weaker than when I was human. I struggled to lift my hand and comfort Rene as the weight of it crushed my spirit as much as my body. He held me steady, and my steps were slow and unsteady, as he began to lead me back to the limousine outside.

My magic, the core of my being, that I had nurtured over years of practice, now flickered like a candle in a gusty wind. I tried to focus on the healing spells I had learned as a child. Even the most basic of incantations slipped from my mind like water through my fingers. One small dart and my magic was a mere shadow of the power that had surged within me.

As Rene helped me sit in the back seat of the limo, and I caught a glimpse of my face in the darkened window, the fragility of my condition became painfully evident. Deep wrinkles were etched on my face, and my once-bright eyes were now dulled by the creeping poison. Beneath the weight of this dark affliction, an ember of determination still burned within me. The sexiest and most powerful creature alive wanted me for eternity. It was a humbling and exciting thought.

I may be weakened, with my magic waning, but I was no stranger to adversity. I had faced daunting odds before, and I refused to succumb to this malevolent poison without a fight. With each labored breath, I gathered my remaining strength, vowing to reclaim the vitality that had been stolen from me. The door to the limo closed and only Rene and I were inside.

"Please Raven. Do not leave me." His voice dripped with pain.

"I will bond with you. But I need to rest. Are we heading to the mansion?" Rene tapped the glass that separated the driver from the back seat.

"No, we are going to a private location. Our bonding site is close to a private cabin I have retained for this very occasion."

My eyes closed as he pulled me against his chest. "Where is this cabin?" My voice was thready, and Rene's arms squeezed my shoulders.

"You will see. Allow me access to your mind. I will place your body in a form of stasis, so the poison does not progress."

"Okay." I felt his mind move in mine, but this was not an invasion. He caressed me from the inside as if he were touching angel wings before the darkness reached for me.

I slowly stirred from my slumber, and the soft sheets surrounded me like a warm cocoon, coaxing me to savor the blissful moments between dreams and reality. A gentle rustle of leaves outside the window alerted me that I was not at the mansion. A faint crackling of a fire from a nearby hearth reminded me of the events that had transpired earlier. My movements were slow as I pushed myself slowly to a sitting position.

Blinking my eyes open, I found myself in a quaint rustic cabin that exuded a modern elegance I hadn't encountered before. The interplay of moonlight filtered through the curtains, illuminating the polished wooden floors. My gaze was drawn toward the carefully curated blend of contemporary and rustic furnishings. The cabin seemed to have a conversation with time itself, capturing the essence of both the old and the new, blending them together in a serene charm.

I appreciated the sensation of crisp linens against my skin as I stretched, searching for the man who had held me when I succumbed to my slumber. The cabin's walls, adorned with tasteful art and muted colors, invited me to enjoy the tranquility they offered, but Rene was not in the room. As I swung my legs over the edge of the bed and let my feet sink into the plush dark rug beneath, I noticed the inviting main room through an open doorway. Modern furniture mingled seamlessly with the cabin's rustic framework, hinting at the harmonious duality of old and new.

Making my way to the window, on bare feet, I marveled at the panoramic view of the surrounding forest. Towering trees swayed to a sacred rhythm, whispering secrets known only to nature's inhabitants. An owl hooted as Rene entered the room with a box in his hand.

"How are you feeling?" he asked as he placed the white parcel on the bed.

"A little better, but the poison is progressing." As beautiful as the cabin was, it could not stop what was happening to me.

"I gave you some of my blood. It has sustained you. But we need to bond for you to have access to my power. I can withstand Dark Dahlia and Belladonna has no effect on me. You need these immunities in order to heal."

"What does the bind do that drinking your blood can't?"

He pulled me back to the bed, and I sat down beside him. "A bond creates a permanent connection that cannot be broken until death. You will gain some of my abilities."

I stared at him for some time. "Will you gain mine? Will you have magic?"

"I don't know. There is no precedence for bonding with a witch."

I frowned. "You understand this could be a one-way street, right?"

He touched my cheek. "I do not need more power, Raven. Only you."

My hand slipped to the box. "What is this?"

He smiled. "In many ways, a binding ceremony is like a marriage. It is customary for a husband to gift his intended with a dress."

"Human women pick their own dresses."

"I am aware. Many clan members choose to have a human wedding as well, and if you wish to have a more formal ceremony later we will."

"Will Jana be here?"

"No. This is a vampire ritual and is sacred to our clan. Only Cassara and Constantine will be present, but I will throw you the wedding of a century for your daughter's benefit."

"Okay. She will love that. So will Isra."

"Thank you, Raven. You have no idea how much your trust means to me."

"Can I see the dress?"

He passed me the simple white box. "I chose this for you myself. But honestly, I do not care what you wear as long as you are mine."

I understood he was telling me that, unlike our huge walk-in closet at the mansion, our personal concierge had not picked this dress. "I'm not sure that closet genie actually exists. I have never seen him."

"He is older and lives on the outskirts of the property and only works for me. You will someday."

I pulled off the top of the box and sucked in a breath. The satin dress was simple, with crystals lining the scooped neckline. My fingers slipped over the shiny material before I picked it up by the straps. "It's stunning." The full-length slim-fitting dress was more than that.

"And yet, it pales in comparison to you." He leaned toward me. "I look forward to taking it off you, though."

My eyes roamed over the sparkling creation. "Pervy and powerful. I'm a lucky girl."

Rene chuckled. "I believe I am the lucky one. Would you like me to help you with the zipper?"

I lowered the magnificent dress back into the box. "Isn't Cass going to help me get ready?"

"The ceremony is in a half hour, Raven. I kept you in stasis until now. The poison will sap your strength quickly, so we must get you ready and meet the others by the river."

"River? Where are we?"

"A private location. This is a personal... retreat. I built this house hoping I would find a woman to share my life with. That was a few hundred years ago."

"Nobody else has stayed here?"

"No. Not even Cassara. In truth, I have never spent more than a few hours here myself."

I stood up and pulled on the beautiful dress. Rene zipped me up, and I tied my hair into a messy bun with a few tendrils falling to my shoulder. When I glanced in the full-length mirror in the corner, I couldn't believe my eyes. Even with no makeup and a twenty-second hairdo, I looked stunning. My skin was paler than when I was human and flawless in every way.

Rene slipped his arms around my waist. "You are a vision. Are you ready?"

"Is it a long walk?"

"Place your arms around my neck."

I did as he asked and as a gust of wind blasted against my face, I was transported to an open clearing beside a tinkling stream. Cassara was standing beside Constantine and while both wore leather outfits, they also had long dressy jackets and silver chains with a medallion around their necks. "Wow."

Cass smiled. "I was about to say the same about you."

The similarity in Constantine and Cassara's outfits was noticeable. "Constantine looks like a death dealer."

Rene shrugged. "Actually, it is Cassara who looks like a warrior. I modeled the death dealers after them."

Cass grunted. "Remember when you wake up to snakes in your bed, that you practically called me a poser."

Constantine put his hand on the small of Cassara's back. It was a proprietary move, and I had to admire his lack of fear. "It is unseemly for a bride's attendee to threaten the groom on the eve of their binding."

Cass rolled her shoulder. "I will do a lot worse to my own groom."

Constantine smiled. "I am certain you will."

Cass stepped away from Constantine and moved to stand in front of me. "Are you ready?"

"Yes. What do I do?"

Cass took out a knife and held it in one hand. "I am going to take your wrist and recite the feminine half of the ceremony. Constantine will do the masculine half for Rene. When the time is right, you will place your palms together."

I nodded as Constantine took hold of Rene's wrist and held it up with his dagger in one hand.

There was no church or special building. Nature coursed around us as if it were a living stadium, waiting for our union, and I glanced at the full moon, trusting Cassara and Constantine.

Cass pointed her dagger to the moon. "It is time."

Constantine pointed his dagger at the moon as both held our wrists. As I stared into Rene's eyes, I glimpsed the loneliness of his life. Those windows to his soul were unending, and I looked forward to breaking the immortal cycle. Still, this ceremony would bond us for all time, and a shiver traced my spine as the breeze fluttered the tendrils of hair against my collarbone.

Rene's presence was intoxicating, with a blend of danger and desire that had attracted me from the moment I saw him. Now we would undergo a connection that transcended time.

Constantine brought the tip of his dagger to Rene's hand. "Rene, do you promise to honor Raven and put her needs before your own? Respect her in all aspects of clan life and treat her as an equal in all things."

"It shall be done," Rene said.

Cass put the tip of her dagger against my palm. "Raven, do you promise to be a partner worthy of Rene? To support him in the days to come and stand by his side no matter the circumstances?"

"I do," I said.

"Do you accept Raven for all her strengths and weaknesses?" Constantine asked.

"Yes," Rene said.

"Raven, do you accept Rene for all his strengths and weaknesses?" Cass asked.

"Yes," I said.

Constantine cut Rene's palm, and the blood dripped down his wrist to Constantine's arm. "I bind thee."

Cass squeezed my wrist before she cut my palm. "I bind thee."

They both let go of our wrists as Rene and I clasp fingers. The ceremony was simple, and I expected there to be some kind of blood exchange. While my palm tingled, there wasn't an instant relief from the grogginess still plaguing my body.

Rene glanced at Constantine. "Thank you, my friend."

He nodded. "She will heal in time, but she is weak in the magical sense and will remain so until your bodies stabilize."

I leaned toward Cass. "What does that mean?"

Cass smiled. "All couples have an adjustment period. It takes time for your blood to fully mingle and your new abilities to emerge."

My eyes narrowed on her. "How many of these ceremonies have you performed?"

Cass grunted. "Con has performed dozens, but this is my first one. I don't get too close to most people."

"Thank you for being my friend, Cass." She glanced away but not before I saw a sadness in her eyes. She was not big on the mushy stuff, but she had been the best friend I ever had next to Isra.

Con winked at me. "Don't mind her Raven. She struggles to let her guard down." He was more right than he knew, but I had the feeling that Constantine wanted a lot more from Cassara than she was willing to give.

"You are very good at this," I said.

He shrugged. "I am usually commended for my fighting skills, so this is a pleasant change."

I shrugged. "I have never seen you fight, but I like you." I leaned in and kissed his cheek before Rene pulled me back to him.

"It is inappropriate for you to flirt with Constantine during our binding ceremony."

Cass turned to look at me before we both laughed.

Constantine shook his head. "I never believed I would see the day."

"What day?" I asked.

Con motioned to Rene. "Him acting like a lovesick puppy. He is too old for such foolishness."

Rene released my hand, and when I looked at my palm, the skin had already healed. "Remember this day, my friend. You will understand when your own bride stands before you."

Constantine smiled. "I look forward to that particular side of crow."

I laughed. "I love this family and I am glad you came to help us, Con. We really needed you."

Cass grunted. "That is true, but don't inflate his ego. It bulges more than his muscles." Her tone was begrudging, but it rung with truth.

Constantine touched her cheek. "You know there is nothing I won't do to ensure your safety."

She stepped back almost reluctantly. "Don't get so sentimental, Con."

Con winked at me. "You see what I am forced to deal with?"

Cassara's jaw dropped. "Since when do you have a sense of humor and where were you hiding it?"

Con turned to her. "There is more about me that you don't know than you do. You fear nothing except me."

Cassara's eyes flickered. "I don't fear you. I will fight anyone."

Con nodded. "You don't fear my blade, Cara."

Cass glanced away, and I admired Constantine even more. I knew Cara meant beloved.

Con motioned toward the forest. "We should head back to the mansion. Shadow Bone clan members are like feral cats when they are not monitored."

Cass grunted, but neither of us could stifle our laughter.

CHAPTER 13

*R*ene held my hand as we got in the back of the limousine and took our seats. His arm snaked around my neck and pulled me against his chest. His fingers traced the exposed skin on my shoulder as Cass took her seat opposite us.

Constantine was last, and he sat so close to Cassara that their thighs were touching. He had room on the other side, but he chose not to give her any space.

She glanced at him with flickering eyes. "Would you like to lie down? You would take up less space."

He turned to her and arched an eyebrow. "I require little sleep, but if you are offering to give me a massage on the way home, then I humbly accept."

Cassara's hand went to her weapon as Rene coughed.

"Constantine, you are playing with fire. I thought you had given up on your death wish."

Constantine shifted slightly in his seat and the material creaked as his leathers rubbed against it. "I have not had such thoughts since Cassara finished her training."

Cass grunted. "Yeah, but you were a total hardass when you

were my mentor. I honestly thought you might kill me some days."

Constantine turned to stare at her. "I ensured you were the best. Few could take you in a fight and I trust every one of those men. I had to ensure your safety since Rene insisted you remain with him."

The muscles ticked in Cassara's jaw, but she was wise enough not to argue. Everything he said was true; only his motives went unsaid.

"Honestly, Cass, I am not sure how you resist him."

Cass blinked before focusing on me. "Excuse me?"

I glanced at Constantine's muscular form and handsome features. "With the exception of Rene, he is the sexiest man I have ever seen."

Cass slipped her hand to her eyes. "Jesus Raven. You can't say that in front of him. His entire head might explode from a comment like that. It can barely contain his ego as it is."

Constantine smiled, and I had to return it. "You are quite fortunate to have such a loving and honest bride."

I laughed as Rene brought my fingers to his lips. "I must agree with you, since she admitted I am more attractive."

Cass threw her hands in the air in exasperation. "What are you, two pre-pubescent boys?"

Constantine leaned toward her. "If anyone could make me feel young again, it is you."

She punched Constantine's arm. "What has gotten into you? Stop it before I stake you."

Constantine laughed. "I always enjoy it when you try."

Cass mumbled something under her breath. "... geezer with a spear."

Constantine's smile faded to be replaced with a look that made me shiver. "We are here, Cass. Are you ready?"

She nodded and her serious face matched Constantine's. "You are Rene's attendant, so you have the honor of announcing their status and how you want them to refer to Raven in formal situations."

Constantine nodded. "I have decided."

He opened the door to the vehicle when it came to a stop and waited for Cass to join him. They stood like sentries at the side of the limo as we exited, then stood shoulder to shoulder as we approached the entrance to the mansion.

Constantine opened the front door and held it for Cass before Rene and I entered. "I wish to announce the entrance of Rene and Raven Roth. They have completed their bonding ceremony and I entreat any who oppose this union to challenge me."

My heart raced as I entered the grand foyer of the opulent mansion with my hand gently clasped in Rene's. All conversation hushed instantly, and the air held an oppressive tension. I had no idea what had transpired while we were gone, but it was obvious they had not expected to see Rene again. At least not alive. Anticipation and fear crackled like electricity as the members of the vampire clan glanced toward the hallway. They were waiting for something... or someone. The silence was palpable, like a collective breath held in suspended animation, as they accepted the undeniable truth of our bonding.

The return of Rene's vitality was a testament to our shared strength and the eternal bond we had completed with the ceremony. His recovery from the treacherous compound killing him was nothing short of miraculous, a testament to his resilience and the depth of our connection. The trial of those events had only solidified our connection, and now we stood before our clan, with our destinies intertwined for all time.

The clan was rendered speechless, despite being used to the subtle changes of power and nuances of politics that coursed through the vampire world. They had witnessed a miracle, from the transformation of a witch to Rene's less-than-subtle courtship of me. The recognition of our bond and my new standing within this clan and every other rippled through the room like a gusting wind.

Hushed chatter broke out around us as Rene and I exchanged a knowing glance. Our silent conversation spoke volumes. We were a united front, two halves of a powerful whole, and ready to face whatever challenges the future would bring. The quiet strength in his gaze mirrored my determination, and was enforced by the two leather-clad sentries that now stood beside us. The clan members were gradually recovering from their surprise, and began to nod respectfully. Most were in a silent show of respect for the connection we had solidified, but whispers of disapproval rustled in the air like leaves in a growing gale storm.

Several clan members darted out of the way as Dimitri entered the foyer. His eyes roamed over Rene in anger before he briefly focused on my dress. "It appears your bonding has stabilized the progression of the disease. I will cancel the assembly immediately."

Rene released my hand. "I told you not to call an assembly. Are you telling me that you ignored a direct order?"

Dimitri flinched under Rene's furious gaze. "You were infected. That compound has killed every other vampire afflicted. I had no way to confirm you were in your right mind."

Rene placed his finger in the middle of Dimitri's chest, and all the chatter ceased. "I am not just any vampire, and you know it. You are a coward and care nothing for this clan or the well-being of our species. You intended to use my attack to gain power. It is pathetic and a childish waste of resources."

Dimitri's lip curled. "I have served this clan admirably and will continue to do so."

Rene grunted. "That is where you are wrong. I was remiss in allowing you to continue as leader."

Dimitri's eyes widened. "I have never betrayed the clan. I have always put its needs first. You cannot demote me, when my descension is so close, anyway."

Cass took my arm and led me from the arguing men to the corner of the room. "Sorry about this. A binding is usually a pleasant time for the clan. Dimitri and his followers are just pissed because you stabilized Rene. He thought Rene's sickness was an opportunity, though he never stood a chance of ascending to overseer."

I stared at Constantine, who remained at Rene's side. "Yeah, I think Con would behead Dimitri before allowing that to happen."

Cass shuddered. "Worse, he would have taken leadership until a suitable replacement was found. There is nobody more suited than Constantine, so it would have been a permanent position."

"Really?"

"Yes, I think..." Cass was flung in the air away from me and smashed into the far wall before crashing to the ground. The shimmering barrier formed around me, effectively cutting me off from the rest of the clan.

The dark shadows twisted and formed inside the barrier with me as Brigid stepped from the dark, evil mist. "I hope you didn't think this pathetic excuse for a union would be allowed to continue."

My power rose within me, but Constantine was right. It was nowhere near as powerful as it had been before I was infected with the witch poison. "You are like a bad penny, Brigid. You keep turning up when we least expect you."

She shrugged. "I brought my friends with me."

"Is this where you attack me?"

She smiled. "In time, but I thought you would like to see that whore vampire friend of yours die first."

Dimitri's brother stepped from a shroud on the opposite side with a look of pure hatred. This was nothing like the easygoing man I had met a couple of days ago. "Time to die, Cass."

I backed away from Brigid, and blasted the barrier, but my magic was not powerful enough to penetrate her shield. I knew I had to conserve my strength and trust Cass and Rene to help one another as several mercenaries exited half a dozen misty shrouds.

Dimitri looked as shocked as the rest of the clan by Davon's betrayal, and he backed away from Rene and Constantine when they turned on the intruders with glowing red eyes.

Brigid smiled. "I took the liberty of confining the rest of the death dealers before we crashed your party. Rene and his leather-clad friend will be forced to fight all of us."

My gaze moved to Cassara and while her eyes appeared open and staring at the center of the room, she hadn't moved. "What did you do to her?"

Brigid shrugged. "I simply hit her with enough force to break every bone in her body. Painful, but she would have healed in time. Davon is here to ensure that doesn't happen."

My heart stuttered. "You came here to kill Cass?"

"Of course not. The vampires are insignificant, except for you. Davon agreed to help us in exchange for Cassara's life. He really hates that bitch. I am here because of you. Rene could become more powerful than any creature who ever lived if you are not removed from this earth. You have no concept of the folly of your actions. He used you to boost his power and now you must die."

Davon advanced on Cassara's inert form. His sneer was a mask of madness. "You should have accepted my proposal, Cass. It was an honor and one I never bestowed on anyone before or after."

He pulled a weapon I didn't recognize from under his tan leather jacket. It looked like a cross between a laser weapon and a dart gun but was different than a UV light as the end consisted of two prongs with electrical sparks arcing between them.

"No," I whispered.

Brigid pulled an identical weapon from beneath her robe. "I wouldn't worry, honey. You will be joining your broken friend."

Constantine beheaded two mercenaries and moved to stand between Cass and Davon as Rene pounded on the shield separating me from the others in the room. "Your time has come to an end, Davon. Your death will serve as a reminder to those who oppose Rene's rule of what happens when you break clan law."

Davon hissed. "You overgrown ass. You are just as bad as Rene. Dimitri will be the next leader of the clans and he will ensure we are not the humans' whipping boys. We hide in the shadows while the humans flourish. The vampires and witches should have more control over the conclave and human law. They are weaker than us."

Constantine rolled his shoulders. "Your madness is only surpassed by your brother's. We were all human Davon. Your idiocy knows no end. But I will relieve you of your life so you may find peace in the next."

Davon aimed his weapon at Constantine, but as he discharged it and a double-pronged electrical arc pummeled toward the ancient vampire, he simply spun to the side and sent a small silver dagger flying through the air.

The strange weapon clattered to the floor as Davon clutched his neck and blood spurted from between his fingers. I had no idea what was on that blade, but vampires were obviously allergic to it.

Constantine approached Davon with the grace of a large feline, before he extended his spear and swiftly arced the sharpened end toward Davon's neck.

Dimitri screamed as the sharp blade separated Davon's head from his neck and the body slumped to the floor.

Rene continued his barrage against the shield, but Davon's death momentarily distracted Brigid, and I sent a small bolt of energy toward her hand. Whatever that weapon was, it looked fatal to vampires, and I had no plans to be an undead guinea pig.

Brigid screamed as the energy hit her wrist, and the strange weapon clattered to the tile floor. Her gaze moved to the door as the remaining death dealers arrived and began to kill or incapacitate the mercenaries. She turned to me with hatred as the shroud formed around her and disappeared a second before the barrier fell and Rene was at my side.

Dimitri dashed to his brother's side and knelt by his body. "No, Davon." There was no mistaking the pain in his voice, and I felt a pang of regret.

Rene stared at the fallen clan member. "He was a traitor."

Dimitri's eyes flashed red as they met Rene's. "You will regret this. You are blind to the wiles of the blood witch. Even her own kind know she is a threat and instead of putting her down like a feral cat, you invite her into your bed."

Rene hissed. "I will allow you to live since you are insane with grief, but my decision about your future as clan head stands. The process of re-selection will begin soon."

Dimitri stood and exited the foyer to complete silence as Constantine moved to scoop Cassara into his arms. He calmly held her as he moved to mine and Rene's side. "Your queen has proven herself worthy of standing beside you, Rene."

I heard his words and the collective gasps, but my gaze was locked on Cassara's face. She had closed her eyes, and I took the hand that draped from Constantine's arms. "Let's get her upstairs."

Constantine nodded. "Of course, my queen."

"I'm not a queen, Con."

"Yes, you are, and if anyone disagrees, I will convince them with my blade."

I shook my head. "No wonder you annoy the crap out of Cass."

His lip twitched as we ascended the stairs toward our suite. "I aim to please."

CHAPTER 14

Constantine stood over Cassara as her shoulder made a cracking noise, and she hissed. "You are healing faster than expected. How long until you are mobile?"

Cass pushed herself to a sitting position in Rene's bed. He had Con place her there, so she was involved in our conversation about Brigid and Davon's treachery. None of us believed Dimitri had suspected his brother was working behind his back, but Davon's motives were clear. He wanted Dimitri in charge. "Get me a glass of blood."

Rene grabbed a bottle from the minibar and poured it before handing it to Constantine. The burly warrior sat at the edge of the bed and held the glass to Cassara's mouth. There was a gentleness to his actions, and Cass wrapped her fingers around his hand.

I sat on the chair in the room, but sighed loudly when Cass released the glass. "Cass, what was Davon talking about? What proposal did you turn down?"

Cass grunted. "After repeated attempts to get me in bed, Dimitri sent his brother with a formal proposal. It outlined bonding with Dimitri and his intention to support me as the next clan leader."

Constantine's eyes flickered. "He proposed a politically-motivated bond?"

Cass nodded. "Can you believe that shit? I told him to take a flying fuck, and he never made any additional overtures after that. Honestly, I never thought more about it until Davon mentioned it. That was over fifty years ago."

Constantine's eyes remained on Cassara as she rolled her shoulder. "Rene, I wish to challenge Dimitri. I know Cassara did not tell you about this proposal, but that was a disgrace. He was attempting to use her position as your personal adviser as a way to retain power. He will seek to align with a weak-minded female that he can control in order to regain power over the clan."

Rene shook his head. "Dimitri is a virtual pariah now. He will never hold any position of power within the clan."

I stood from the chair. I had changed from my beautiful dress to simple black capris and a white blouse with a tan jacket, while Cass was healing. "That could make him more dangerous. He has nothing to lose."

Con turned to me. "Do you believe he will attack Rene? He is no match for him physically."

Cass pushed on Con's shoulder, forcing him to move before she got up from the bed. She pulled off the long formal leather jacket that signified her as my attendant for the ceremony. Her leather tank top was tucked into her belt, adorned with various weapons. "Dimitri won't go after Rene. He will go after Raven. Once he rebounds from his brother's death, she will be his target."

Con shrugged off the long leather jacket that matched Cassara's and tossed it on the bed. "He will die painfully if he comes anywhere near her." His muscles bulged, and I pursed my lips before Cass gave me a dirty look.

"Don't say it, Raven."

"I wasn't... it's just there is a lot you could do with..."

"He basically decreed that everyone in every clan refer to you as the queen. We don't call Rene king, so you technically have more power than he does."

"Wh... what?" I stammered. My eyes moved to Rene. "That isn't true, right?"

Con shrugged. "It is."

My jaw dropped, and I placed both hands on my hips. "Why would you do something so stupid? Everyone practically hates me already."

Cass sighed. "Because Rene would turn into something that even Constantine couldn't stop if you died. With Rene's evolution at hand, you are the only thing that can keep him sane through it. You are the most important vampire alive."

I blew out a breath. "No pressure."

Rene walked over and kissed my cheek. "Do not concern yourself with..."

The entire mansion shook, and the chandelier danced in the room. Constantine and Cass grabbed their weapons, but the vibrations stopped right before the shouting. Cass grabbed her phone before hissing.

"There was an explosion in the training facility. Val and Quinn want us down there now," Cass said.

Con opened the door. "Cass, you flank. We take no chances with Raven's life."

I expected Cass to balk at the order, but she nodded her ascension without a flicker of irritation.

Con disappeared into the hallway before Rene guided me through the exit. There was nobody on the upper floor and Cass followed after us with her staff in her hand, though it wasn't extended.

We made our way down the stairs and to the hall to the training facility, but I inhaled the smell of burnt wood before we entered the massive room.

As I stepped through the large door of the training facility, my heart squeezed at the horrifying sight. The place the death dealers had used as a sanctuary for honing their skills was now engulfed in orange flames that consumed the walls and sent black smoke billowing into the air. It replaced the familiar scent of wood and metal with the malevolent stench of destruction.

The exterior wall bore a gaping hole that looked as though it had been hit with a missile, shattering the concrete and metal like fragile glass. I froze as my eyes took in the surreal scene. The majority of the training center had been ripped apart, leaving behind only chaos and devastation. Cass made a strangled noise as her eyes moved over the loss of her personal sanctuary.

The training apparatus that had once stood proudly beneath the massive, vaulted ceiling now lay buried beneath mounds of debris and rubble. The place where Cass had spent countless hours training her death dealers, perfecting their techniques, and forging unbreakable bonds with her team was now reduced to a heap of smoking ruins.

It scattered broken and partially-burned weapons across the charred floor, their usually gleaming edges now dulled by the fire's touch. These tools had once been wielded with precision and finesse and seeing them in such disarray was like a punch to the gut. Cass looked like she was ready to skewer whoever was responsible and she had Constantine to back her up. His face was a mask of fury.

Val approached her with his hand on his weapon. He was forced to sidestep a pile of rubble. "Nobody was hurt, but the integrity of the exterior wall is compromised. We will need a human crew if we want debris removal and construction to continue during the day."

Rene's jaw ticked. "I do not want anyone on site that we can't trust. Who is responsible for this?"

Val's lips pursed. "Brigid blasted the wall, but Dimitri met with her and left with over fifty clan members. They have fled the mansion."

Rene's eyes flickered red. "What?"

Val glanced at Constantine, whose eyes blazed with red fire. "Several clan members witnessed Dimitri talking to Brigid after she magically bombed us. Then they all left."

"He joined the dark faction?" I whispered.

Constantine glanced at the smoking hole in the wall. "The witch played us."

Cass and Rene glanced down and while they seemed to know what Constantine was talking about, I didn't. "What does that mean?"

Con clipped his staff back on his belt. "Davon was a traitor, but he had no political pull, nobody who would follow him."

My eyes widened. "She used Davon to get to Dimitri."

Cass nodded. "Every kill was meant to seed frustration and discord. She chose vampires that would upset the clan and ensure they wanted new leadership. Dimitri already had a massive following and many of the clan believed Rene was on the brink of madness. He wasn't a traitor... until we killed his brother."

Constantine shook his head. "She manipulated Dimitri as easily as her own coven."

Rene's face hardened. "I want a list of every vampire who left with Dimitri. Once they take action against us, they will be considered traitors, and every warrior and death dealer will hunt them until they are dust upon the earth."

Rene grabbed my hand and led me from the smoking room as Constantine and Cass followed behind us. He said nothing as he led me to the foyer, where dozens of vampires stood with shocked faces. Some had smudges of smoke and they looked as if their entire world was about to collapse.

When he stopped at the edge of the hallway and scanned the

room, I leaned toward him. "What do you mean by take action against us?"

Rene raised his voice. "Once a vampire turns on his or her clan, they have broken our laws. There may be those who have been misguided or threatened into leaving with Dimitri the traitor. If any clan member returns before unsanctioned actions against their clan, then there will be no punishment imposed. As it stands, any who oppose us are under a death sentence to be carried out by the death dealers or the warriors."

Several well-dressed clan members stared at Constantine, but it was a young vampire who spoke up. "The warrior is staying here?"

Constantine stared at the tiny man with open hostility. "This clan is a disgrace. Rene has been far too lenient with your political stupidity. I will bring more warriors from the Shadow Phantom Clan to ensure both Rene and Raven's safety and to restore order to this traitorous clan. I will not tolerate this uprising."

The young man who spoke up stepped back. "Can we contact the people who left with your permission? Try to get them to return?"

Rene nodded. "Email them or use whatever means necessary to get them to see reason. Constantine has my full support. They have little time. Once Dimitri acts against us, this concession is over."

The quiet in the room was palpable and Cass stared at the floor as if she had personally failed Rene. While he would never see it that way, Constantine's eyes were on Cassara as well. Hurting the clan was one thing, but making Cass feel like she had failed was something else. Dimitri had made the deadliest enemy on earth, and I had no desire to witness the pain that traitor would endure.

Rene's cell phone made me jump as he pulled it from his

jacket before reading the text. "Manu thinks he has found the last page. Val, is the conference room still intact?"

Val nodded. "Only the training facility was damaged. It was hit in the center of the exterior wall, so as long as we avoid this room, we should be okay."

I touched Rene's arm. "I can use magic to reinforce the conference room." I thought about the destruction. "It would take more power to fix the training facility with magic than manually, though."

CHAPTER 15

*M*anu was waiting in the conference room when we entered, but he wore a surgical mask over his face, and I was sure it was to block the smell of smoke in the air. Normally, the large room was littered with artifacts and scrolls he was inspecting, but a single piece of parchment lay on the long table. The crack in one wall displayed the effects the blast had on neighboring walls and the thick striation in the drywall exposed a wooden beam.

The attractive man pointed at the paper on the table. "I know where the next page is."

Rene nodded. "Where is it?"

"The monster hunter's cave, only I am not sure exactly where it is located. It would have been abandoned centuries ago, but I believe there is a hidden passageway in their former stronghold."

Rene's lip curled slightly. "I know where the cave is. I emptied it myself after the sect was disbanded."

I squeezed Rene's arm. "Their stronghold was close to here?"

Rene nodded. "They have a few, but the one closest to us was in the mountains just outside Black Blossom County. There is a network of tunnels in there and most would never find their caverns."

Manu's eyes brightened. "You can get us in?"

Rene nodded. "We must leave now in order to return to the vehicle before the sun comes up."

I stared at Manu. "Do you ever sleep?"

He winked at me. "I sleep during the day. My father says I am practically a vampire already."

Rene motioned to the door. "Follow us in your vehicle. Would you like Cassara to ride with you? She is familiar with the area we plan to visit."

Manu nodded. "I would like that, provided that monstrosity of a vampire doesn't try to behead me for riding with her."

Rene's lip twitched. "Constantine does not kill indiscriminately."

Manu grunted. "Excuse me if I don't take your word for it. But have you seen the way he looks at her? I will never tease that woman again."

Rene was quiet for some time. "Constantine trained Cassara. He is... protective of her."

Manu rolled the ancient piece of parchment paper. "It's more than that, but I will meet her out front. We will follow your limousine."

"We will be taking an all-terrain vehicle."

Rene and I exited the conference room, with Manu following us. Cass was already waiting in the foyer and Con gave Manu a disapproving look as we approached.

"Be nice. He is helping us," I whispered to the large warrior.

His lip twitched, but he nodded gracefully. "Of course, my queen."

I rolled my eyes. "I see why Cass wants to stake you."

Cass laughed and winked at me. "This is why I like you."

Con sighed. "I admit Raven has a certain appeal. Shall I drive you in the vehicle or do you wish me to follow you?"

Rene arched an eyebrow. "I am capable of protecting myself and my woman. Cassara will be with us."

Constantine stared at Rene without expression. "We both know I will not allow you off this property without an escort until we have neutralized this rebellion."

I had to admire Constantine's nerve. Few would openly defy Rene like that. I would say that he was the male version of Cass, but Constantine was far older and Rene's oldest friend. He probably taught Cass how to handle the overseer and keep him on his toes.

Rene motioned toward the door. "You can ride with us, Con, but you need to work on your people skills."

"Why?" Con asked as he followed Rene and me toward the door.

Cass grunted. "And you thought I was bad. Con has the tact of a bull in a china shop."

I was still shaking my head as we exited the mansion to find a large four-wheel-drive Bronco with blacked-out windows. "Wow."

Cass smirked. "I love that vehicle. I'm bummed I am with Manu."

A dark-blue dune buggy pulled up behind the black Bronco, and Cass whistled. "Well, color me impressed. Manu has some tricked-out wheels."

Cass jogged ahead and got in the passenger's seat of Manu's dune buggy, but he cast a leery glance at Constantine as the large warrior got into the driver's seat. Rene and I got into the back, and we pulled away from the mansion, with Cass and Manu following us.

We drove through the forest, and I was completely lost before

Constantine took a path so grown over the branches scratched the side of the vehicle.

"You are going to need a new paint job after this."

"Probably. The cave entrance is just ahead," Rene said.

With the crunch of gravel beneath the tires, Constantine brought the Bronco to a halt. My heart thumped with a mixture of anticipation and fear as I stared at the entrance of the cave nestled amidst the dense forest. The air was thick with mystery, and an aura of time's passage hung over the deserted and overgrown area. Shafts of moonlight pierced through the wavering canopy, casting dappled shadows that danced like ancient spirits on the forest floor.

The Bronco's engine ticked as soon as Constantine turned it off. It was the only sound that dared to break the eerie silence. The entrance of the cave beckoned like a portal to another world where stories of a brutal past prayed to be rediscovered.

With a mixture of trepidation and determination, I swung open the door and slipped to the ground. My thick-soled boots sank into the earth, reminding me I was a visitor in this natural oasis. The cave's mouth yawned wide, revealing a tunnel that seemed to lead into the heart of the mountain. The jagged rock walls were rugged and worn, a testament to the passage of time and the eons they had endured.

As I approached the entrance, a shiver traced my spine, both from the coolness emanating from the cave and the realization we would discover another piece of the prophecy. My prophecy. Manu pulled up behind us and exited with his flashlight, directing its beam into the gaping darkness.

The light's reach was limited, but I no longer required its help. The remnants of ancient symbols etched into the walls were plain to me, but their meaning was lost to the ages. The uneven ground beneath me crunched as I moved deeper into the cave, accompanied by my friends. I felt a surge of exhilaration mingled with fear, hoping the latest revelation would help us in our bid to save the vampires and stop a war.

Rene led us through a series of tunnels, but after a few minutes, they all looked the same. He didn't stop until we were inside a massive cavern with nothing but sand for a floor. "This is it."

I glanced around. "There is nothing here."

Rene pointed to the center of the room. "This was their training area. There are several smaller rooms where the hunters lived and raised their children. Males were trained for combat and the females were traded to other hunter families to strengthen bloodlines."

Cass grunted. "Breeding stock. Great."

Manu was already running his hand over the rough walls. "Look for a lever or a hole you can place your hand in. If there is nothing here, we will start checking the living quarters."

Rene began to shuffle his feet in the sand. "It will be here. They revered their training area. The personal space was meager in comparison. They didn't even value their male children until the boys proved they had a certain level of skill."

Cass and I inspected the walls with Manu as Constantine and Rene shuffled through the sandy floor. It was over an hour before Constantine went over the same area three times. "There is an unusual rock under the sand."

Cass frowned. "It's a cave. They likely placed the sand here themselves to have a softer training area."

Rene shook his head. "The hunters preached toughness. They would not haul sand into a cave to create a softer training area."

Constantine went to his knees as Rene did the same. They scooped handfuls of sand from the floor to reveal a smooth, circular rock. It had several symbols etched on the top and appeared to be sealed well. "Is this it?"

Manu leaned over the chiseled rock face. "I think so. We can't be sure unless we are able to open it. Are you strong enough to break the seal on..."

Constantine grabbed one side of the rock that appeared to act as a lid. There was a crunching sound as he pulled the circular top off and tossed it to the corner of the room as if it were a granite disc.

Cass grunted. "Show off."

Constantine ignored her and peered into the chiseled rock tube. "It appears to be a well. They must have connected with an underground spring. This was their water source. They covered it with sand to hide it."

Cass glanced around. "A water source in the middle of a training room. They cast their weapons here. This is a forge... or it was."

Rene stood. "You are right. This room was full of weapons when I... decommissioned this place."

I swallowed hard. "What happened to the monster hunters?"

Rene turned to me. "I killed the men and delivered the women and children to a local baron I trusted. The women were happy about the change in lifestyle, as they were not allowed to leave the cave. The older male children were less impressed with the changes."

Manu dipped his hand in the water. "Damn, that is cold. I would make bets the page is at the bottom. Hopefully they sealed it properly. I would hate to go down there for nothing."

Cass began to remove her weapons belt. "You aren't going down there. I don't need to breathe, and the cold is irrelevant. Besides, the rest of you won't fit."

She was right. Her lithe frame was an asset in this case, and she wouldn't have a difficult time swimming to the bottom and reversing backward. I was glad she offered, because I shuddered at the thought of a black tube.

Constantine stood beside her as she removed her shirt. The

black bra beneath was simple cotton, as was her underwear when she removed her boots and pants. "Your undergarments will not hinder you."

Cass rolled her eyes. "I wasn't planning on giving you a show."

"Perhaps another time," Con said without emotion.

"You wish," Cass said as she swung her legs into the well. "I was going to swim down, but I think it would be easier to weight myself and fall to the bottom. Then I can release the stone and swim back up."

"That is a sound plan," Rene said as he grabbed a loose rock from the wall and handed it to Cass.

She clutched it to her chest and popped into the well as a splash of water erupted above her.

My heart squeezed as the surface of the water smoothed over and not a single bubble breached the surface. While my mind understood she didn't need to breathe, and the deeper she went down, the less likely she was to send ripples to the surface. My body clenched beneath my clothes and my anxiety spiked.

A ripple wavered over the top of the well seconds before Cass crested the surface. Her hand exited the water as Constantine reached for her and hauled her from the well. The metal cylinder was thick and rusty, but she handed it to Manu, before wiping the water from her eyes. Constantine stood so close to her the water rolled down his leather clothing and pooled on the sand at his feet.

Manu tried not to stare at Cassara's sleek, sexy form, but no man was immune to her lure with slicked-back hair and pale skin. But he glanced away when he found Constantine glaring at him. His eyes reverted to the metal rod. "How do we open it? If there were any symbols on it, they have long since disintegrated."

Con held out his hand. "May I see it?"

Manu passed him the rod, and Constantine took a small vial

from his belt. He poured it over the rusty pipe and bubbles erupted around the rim.

"What is that?" I asked.

Cass motioned to the bubbling pipe. "That compound is used to etch metal. It should erode the rust and debris. Then we can see if there are any markings."

When the majority of the bubbling stopped, Constantine dipped the pipe in the water and retracted it. There were bits of shiny area exposed beneath the rust now, but a thin line was revealed at one end of the metal rod. I pointed to it. "That must be the opening. How do we break the seal?"

Constantine clutched the pipe and squeezed, the metal beneath the cap making a wrenching noise before he gripped the cap with his other hand and pulled it off.

Manu whistled. "I didn't realize vampires were that strong."

Cass shrugged. "Our strength in our undead body is reflective of our human one. Constantine is almost as strong as Rene. He is more of a showoff, though."

Constantine stared at Cassara as he passed the pipe to Rene. "You should read the passage."

Rene took the pipe and gently pulled the paper from the inside out. He unfurled it slowly and his eyes moved over the ancient script.

"What does it say?" I asked.

He was silent for a few minutes. "This confirms you are the blood witch."

My shoulders sank, and I stared at the floor. "Of course it does." Rene touched my shoulder gently. "This page tells you to accept your destiny as the blood witch. It is not the dark omen we assumed it to be. This says you are the protector of the vampire race and holder of the king's heart. That only you can help the king survive what is coming."

"What?"

Constantine sighed. "She is as we hoped. The anchor for the king."

Rene nodded. "I knew she was mine the moment I saw her, but I have no way of confirming she will anchor me."

Manu frowned, flicking his beam between us. "What are you talking about?"

Cass moved to stand in front of Manu. "It won't be a secret for long, but Rene is... going through a transformation. I trust you will keep this to yourself until we have more information."

Manu nodded. "I would never betray you or Rene, but what is this transformation? What does it do to him?"

Cass shook her head. "We don't know. Raven is the holder of the king's heart. She is the only one who can keep him... stable and balance his power during this process. None of us know what a true king is or what Rene will transform into. The previous overseers went mad during the process."

Manu motioned to the page. "Is there anything else?"

Rene nodded. "The witches want Raven dead because they know she is the only one who can stabilize me. They are scared I will become more powerful than them with access to magic." He stared at the page. "This page ends mid-sentence. There is another."

Manu stepped forward, making his flashlight bob in the dark. "Do you know where it is?"

Rene pointed to a symbol of a fire. "The hearth. My guess is the private cavern of the hunter leader."

CHAPTER 16

"*W*here is the private cave for the hunter leader?" I asked.

Rene glanced back the way we had come. "The personal caves are further into the mountain. I did not remove those implements."

Rene placed the page back inside the metal tube and handed it to Manu. "Come with me."

He grabbed my hand and led us through a series of intersecting tunnels. Explorers had likely found these caves, but Rene had only concerned himself with weapons from the Monster Hunter sect.

I didn't even realize we were in a personal cave when Rene stopped. "This is it."

My gaze roamed around the small room as Manu's flashlight illuminated the walls. Unlike the sandy floor of the training room that hid the forge, they chiseled the floor of this cavern, smoothing the rock. While they had evened out the more jagged pieces on the floor, it was still quite rough. "Did they have beds?" I couldn't see any sign of a structure.

Manu knelt down and pulled a tattered piece of cloth from the ground. "Tanned leathers. They lay on the floor on their version of a bedroll."

Rene stared at the walls. "It was simply fur rugs with a cooking area in the center. The leader had a few items in here. It was his wife and child's responsibility to cook for him and maintain their domicile."

Cass grunted. "I know it was a different time, but being treated like cattle is wrong no matter the century."

Constantine began to kick loose gravel from the chiseled rock. "They buried their forge. It seems reasonable they would bury other valuables."

We all began kicking loose gravel but after a half hour we had covered the entire floor with no result. Manu was moving over the sidewalls of the cavern and stopped when he found a slight indentation. "This impression is packed with the same sand we found in the training cavern."

Cass moved to the small hole. "No man could get their hand in there. We may have to take the wall down."

I moved toward the wall. And placed my hand against the rock. "No need. I can separate the sand and rock and retrieve the scroll, provided it is only an inch or two from the surface."

Cass motioned for me to try, and I placed my hand inside the hole.

My fingers sunk into the top layer of sand, but I felt nothing resembling a pipe before my power snaked out from my fingers, searching with tiny tendrils of magic beneath my hand. The ping was instant, and I wrapped my power around the object before lifting it from its shallow grave. It levitated as it exited the hole and dropped into my other hand.

Constantine shifted slightly, and I passed him the metal tube that matched the one from the forge.

He didn't use the etching compound on this one as it was less rusty than the first one, because of the dark, dry conditions, but it made the same wrenching noise as he squeezed just beneath the cap and broke the seal. He passed the pipe to Rene once he took off the lid.

Rene removed the page and scanned its contents. "This goes on where the other page ends. It says the Blood Witch will have the ability to share her magic with her king once she matures. That the king will be able to do the same. This has..." he trailed off as we stared at him.

I touched his shoulder. "What is it?"

"This warns of the king, but not the one bonded to the Blood Witch. This explains that only the true overseer must survive and only if he has the faith of his bride. Only he can protect the human realm from the usurper."

"The usurper?" I asked.

Rene's eyes continued to roam over the script. "There are a few symbols I don't recognize. Manu will need to do more research, but I believe he is a king."

"A vampire king?" I asked.

Cass froze. "Are you insinuating that a vampire overseer is still alive somewhere?"

Rene frowned. "I don't know. I can't confirm the death of any overseer except Siam."

Manu flashed his light on Rene. "How could a previous overseer take leadership without killing the current overseer?"

Rene shook his head. "Perhaps some kind of spell. If the clans believed the overseer was dead, they would select another. My power comes from age and experience, not because I have a title. I can call on my people as their designated overseer, though. If there were suddenly two of us, I fear for the repercussions."

Cass growled. "Since he would be older than you by thousands of years, he would be stronger."

Rene rubbed his chin. "Theoretically, yes, but he would not be accustomed to modern times, and he would not have a bride to stabilize him. Madness does not diminish his power, but his reasoning would continue to degrade."

Constantine turned to Manu. "You will begin investigating this possibility immediately. Look for any information that suggests a prior overseer was... imprisoned or put in some form of stasis instead of murdered. We must confirm this prophecy is false before the clans find out about it."

Manu nodded. "Of course, but I will need access to all scrolls and prophecies concerning the ancient king."

"You will have it. We should return to the mansion before dawn." We all followed Rene when he led us from the caves.

I leaned toward Rene. "How can we claim this new information is false when it's attached to the Blood Witch prophecy? Obviously, I am very real."

Rene's hand squeezed mine. "I am aware."

The opulent foyer was completely empty when we arrived back at the mansion and Cass glanced at Rene. "That is a first."

Rene nodded. "They are mourning the loss of our members. I sense a couple have returned, but most have chosen to stay with Dimitri. He has brainwashed his followers into believing the time of madness is upon me."

Constantine growled low. It was a terrifying sound. "Then declare them traitors. Why wait if you already have your answers? It is time to declare war on this dark faction and any who follow them."

Rene sighed. "Cass, call everyone to the foyer. We will have a clan meeting."

Cass went to an intercom on the wall by the front door. "Everyone in the mansion to the foyer now. This is a direct order."

The sound of doors opening and closing precluded the rush of well-dressed vampires entering the foyer. After a few minutes, several members arrived in sleep attire and had simply thrown on a robe to attend the meeting.

Rene moved to the front of the door, so he was standing before the throng of Shadow Bone members. "Has every deserter been contacted? And given the chance to return? If you have not heard back from your fellow clan members, please speak up."

Rene nodded sadly when the silence stretched between him and the clan. "I declare those not with us today as traitors. We must declare war on the dark faction as well as the witch who leads it. Any who follow her will be terminated."

Florence stepped forward with uncertainty plain on her face. "What about a clan head? Will you start the reselection process?"

"As Dimitri is dead to us, a new permanent clan leader will be chosen. Constantine will head this clan until you choose your replacement. I will approve all initiates personally and call an election when you have at least three suitable candidates selected."

A young man I had seen with Dimitri stepped forward. "The clan has always chosen its candidates. Have protocols changed?"

Rene's eyes flickered. "Of course they have. We have a rogue faction full of vampires led by a witch. The humans have every right to turn on both the empowered and vampire species. We have broken the accords and unless the candidates prove their top priority is our survival, I will not accept their candidacy."

I glanced at Constantine and despite his new elevation, he looked angrier than ever. I winked at him and noticed several members gasp. The young man who had been speaking looked at me like I had lost my mind.

"He is really very sweet," I said before I considered Constantine may not like me defending him.

Cass grunted and covered her mouth. "Only to you, honey."

Constantine gave Cassara a dirty look but remained quiet.

The young man swallowed nervously. "How do we stop the attacks? Now that the dark faction has been discovered, they will inundate us with that poisonous compound."

I leaned toward Rene. "Buy up all the Star Canyon. If they don't have the plant, they can't make more. It isn't something they can mass produce. The seeds are too rare."

Rene nodded. "We will ensure the supply of the compound is very limited, but until we put the rebel witch down, protective protocols will remain in place."

Florence nodded. "What about the vampires that have turned to Dimitri's cause? They continue to try and recruit those within the clan. They will try the others soon."

Rene's eyes narrowed. "Dimitri has attempted to get you to join his rebellion? Since he left the clan?"

Several vampires nodded while others looked around, just as curious of the answer as Rene was.

Florence sighed. "He asked me to train the fledglings he took with him. The young are impressionable, and it pains me to admit we have failed them."

My eyes roamed the cluster of vampires until they rested on Julian. There was a sense of relief that the man Rene and I had chosen together had stayed with the clan. It made me wonder how deep the betrayal of those who left Rene was on the overseer's soul.

Several other clan members regaled stories of Dimitri contacting them and trying to convince them that Rene was on the brink of madness and that a stable leader must be chosen. That the new leader must be a member of Shadow Bone, or the other clans will consume them.

Rene hissed. "That is pure idiocy. His actions could incite another clan war. Us fighting against ourselves will ensure our destruction. Things are not as they once were. The humans outnumber us a thousand to one, but if we tip that balance, we ensure our starvation."

Rene's jaw ticked. "What of Dimitri's brother? What made Davon turn against the clan?"

Val stepped forward. "Quinn and I have been looking into Davon's activities since his betrayal. I don't believe Dimitri knew that his brother was working behind his back to depose you. Davon was reported to be in the Shadow Demon clan the month before his return to Shadow Bone, but when we checked with the clan head, they reported Davon was never there."

Rene huffed. "He was busy conspiring against us."

Val nodded. "It appears so."

Rene rolled his shoulders. "Then Constantine was correct. Brigid used Davon to bring Dimitri to her cause. He allowed his fear of losing power within this clan to cloud his judgment."

I stared up at Rene. "What do we do now?"

CHAPTER 17

*S*everal clan members began to speak at once and Rene held up his hand to still the confusion and fear.

"I assure you that Constantine and I will answer all your questions. We wish to gather any additional information on Dimitri and those who left with him. We will be looking for any clues as to their whereabouts and appreciate your willingness to help." Rene lowered his voice before he leaned toward me. "This will take some time. Why don't you and Cass check on the training facility and see how debris removal is progressing before you retire to our suite? I will join you later."

Constantine touched Cassara's shoulder. "You will remain with Raven until Rene returns to their suite."

Cassara's eyes flickered. "I had no intention of leaving her, numbskull. I have been protecting her since the moment I saw her."

Constantine stared at her without emotion. "Normally, you retiring to your adjoining suite would have sufficed. But I do not trust anyone in this clan to protect Raven except you and Rene."

The anger on her features softened. "I only trust the death

dealers and a few others myself, but don't tell me how to do my job."

Constantine's lip twitched slightly. "I wouldn't dream of it."

Cass moved toward me and motioned with her head. I kissed Rene on the cheek and followed her into the hallway. "Constantine, better get his head out of his ass if he expects to wake up tomorrow."

I was silent for a moment. "He doesn't want to be the clan leader. He looked irritated by the promotion."

"True. He declined leadership at Shadow Phantom. He is only doing this out of duty, and everyone knows it. Con hates political clans."

The hallway was empty as the majority of the clan was in the foyer, but Cassara's death dealers had already returned to the cleanup. Dawn was fast approaching, and they would be forced to avoid the other wall once the sunlight began to stream through.

Cass opened the door to the training room, and we entered to survey the death dealer's progress.

As I stopped in the doorway of the training facility, my heart carried a mix of anticipation and sadness. The damaged room was a testament to the resilience of those who spent hours in this sacred space honing their skills. The acrid scent of smoke had faded, but the charred remnants lingered like a malicious memory etched in the walls.

The room had transformed from the chaotic wreckage of my last visit to some semblance of order. The debris that had covered the floor like an apocalyptic battlefield had been painstakingly cleared, revealing the charred but sturdy floorboards underneath. Shafts of moonlight streamed in through the hole in the wall, illuminating the ring that had seen so many trials of combat.

The seasoned death dealers I had begun to train beside moved with purpose amidst the controlled chaos. They worked in harmony, their strength and unity evident as they utilized their supernatural strength to haul away charred beams and broken training apparatuses. The clatter of metal and broken wood echoed as they dropped the remnants in a pile outside the gaping hole. Val relayed orders to the team about what items he wanted removed next. Their studious response was a reminder of the camaraderie that had always been the foundation of this place.

The walls still bore the scars of smoke damage. A reminder of the inferno that had threatened to consume the mansion and everyone in it. But there was still beauty in the way the moonlight caressed the charred beams, turning those wretched scars into a story of survival. It was as if the very essence of the death dealers had seeped into this facility, leaving an indelible mark that no fire could erase.

As we stepped further into the room, I felt a surge of pride and determination overcome me. This place, though altered by the flames, was still alive with the spirit of those who had refused to be defeated. The death dealers, with their determined brows and dirt-streaked faces, were a living embodiment of strength in the face of adversity. Protectors of the clan until the bitter end.

We walked over to Kirnen, lending a hand to move the remnants of a broken beam. For Cass, it wasn't about cleaning up the debris; it was reclaiming her haven. The scars on the walls and the smell of smoke lingering in the air were a reminder that we were warriors who had weathered the storm and emerged stronger despite our enemies' efforts to destroy us.

I worked alongside my fellow death dealers, and a renewed sense of purpose blossomed within me. Their super-speed was a blessing, but they couldn't always use it when maneuvering the larger pieces of debris. Cass moved to help Val and Quinn with a piece of trellis that had fallen to the floor while I helped Kirnen with a wooded wall that had once belonged to the obstacle course.

He smiled sadly at me. "I am sorry about this, Raven. It all seems so unfair."

I repositioned the charred wood we were angling toward the hole in the wall so we could toss it on the pile outside. "Don't apologize for people's prejudice. That caused this mess."

Kirnen and I tossed the charred wall outside and I moved toward another burn pile. "You misunderstand. I am sorry you died."

I frowned as I turned toward him. "I'm not. At least not anymore. I am sure there will be difficult times in the future, but that is a part of life. Even an undead one."

He pulled his staff from his belt as a barrier formed between us and the other death dealers in the trashed facility. "Dimitri is coming for you. Go quietly and I will not be required to kill you."

Cassara's shout alerted me that Dimitri and his cohorts had returned, and the clash of fighting echoed around us. My gaze remained firmly locked on Kirnen and I was aware he possessed more skill as a death dealer than I did. His slice to my neck had proved that, but he did not possess magic. Even though I was not at full strength, I figured we were evenly matched with my power making up for his superior skill.

"If you raise that blade to me, you are dead. Rene will slaughter you. Don't betray the clan because Dimitri is set on a vendetta."

Kirnen sighed. "It is not Dimitri. I was a historian. I studied the ancient kings and the results of their madness. Rene was good and just overseer, but so were most of the others before the madness began to take root. It is not his fault, but he cannot be allowed to evolve any further."

My fangs lengthened. "Who are you to decide Rene's evolution? Dimitri simply doesn't want to lose power. He will do anything to become overseer."

Kirnen nodded. "Yes, but he is young by our standards and has over a thousand years before he will be considered unsafe to mature."

I stepped back and raised my hands. I hadn't grabbed a weapon, so my magic was all I had. "You are intent on this course of action?"

Kirnen nodded. "I am truly sorry, Raven. If you will not surrender, I must kill you to send Rene into full madness. He is too strong to kill while he is sane, and the longer you live, the slower his progression will be."

I huffed as growls and shouts continued to erupt around me. "You have no idea what his evolution will be. I know this because he doesn't either. There has never been a stable king, because those who aged didn't have an anchor."

Kirnen grunted. "You think because Rene bonded with you, he is stable? You are wrong. Nothing can stabilize a king. The power that starts the transformation drives them mad. Immortality comes at a price. And every vampire must eventually pay. The lycans found this out the hard way. It is time we learned our lesson." He raised his staff before his spear extended and he took a fighting stance.

My eyes searched the surrounding scene as I braced for Kirnen's attack. The facility that had once been a sanctuary for training and camaraderie was now a battleground, echoing with the clash of weapons and the angry shouts of the death dealers. My heart squeezed with a mix of adrenaline and concern coursing through my body.

The death dealers all fought with a fierce determination that sent shivers down my spine, but their sadness at Kirnen's betrayal would run deep no matter the outcome. Their movements were fluid and calculated, like the deadly dance of a gazelle that conveyed the years they had spent honing their skills within these very walls. The clang of steel against steel echoed through the air, punctuated by the occasional groan or scream as the mercenaries were picked off one by one.

Despite the chaos, I noticed the shimmering bubble at the

entrance of the facility. It was some kind of barrier spell, a powerful enchantment that kept the happening within the training facility segregated from the rest of the mansion. The dark magic hummed in the air, a reminder of the potent power of the traitorous witch who wielded it.

My gaze swept across the room, searching for a figure that would stand out among the battle-hardened warriors. Brigid, the traitorous witch who had once been a coven sister, was conspicuously absent. The uncertainty sent a slither of unease through me. Her absence was a mystery that gnawed at my thoughts as I glanced back at Kirnen.

His foot shifted slightly before he swung his weapon in my direction, and I dismissed the errant witch as I unleashed my magic on the opponent before me. The death dealers around me fought with a shared purpose, a unity that had been forged through years of training, purpose, and loyalty. I had to remain vigilant, and I deflected Kirnen's spear with a quick protection spell while scanning for any sign of Brigid.

"Raven!" Cass yelled.

I didn't dare look at her as Kirnen circled me, looking for an opening. "Find Brigid. We need to break her barrier. The rest of the clan can't get near us. She has isolated me. So I assume she is on your side of this bubble." Brigid was smart. She had segregated me from the death dealers and the death dealers from the door. Compartmentalizing your magic like that was difficult, and it spoke of her skill.

"We can't find her, but there are more mercenaries than cockroaches," Cass yelled.

This had to be Brigid's final stand, and I heard Dimitri yell before my steps faltered.

"Kill Cassara. If we eliminate her and Raven, Rene will crumble. He is too attached to the women."

Cass moved at the corner of my vision to stand in front of

Dimitri. "You are such a pussy, Dimitri. You stand here ordering others to kill me when you aren't willing to do it yourself."

Dimitri smiled as a barrier formed between him and Cass. Brigid was hidden in her effective shroud, but she was watching every event and protecting her asset. "Raven is the cause of Davon's death. Her arrival was the beginning of the end. It doesn't need to be this way, Cass. At least not for you. Come with me. Denounce the mad king."

Cass twirled her extended spear. "I would rather suntan in the middle of the day. You are pathetic, Dimitri. Brigid would kill you in a heartbeat if you had one."

"There is nobody to help you, Cassara. Brigid has ensured that the clan is blissfully unaware you are under attack and more mercenaries are arriving by the second beneath her shroud."

It was the same spell Brigid had used when I was attacked at the store. Cass had stared at Powerful Petals, only a few feet away, unaware of the events transpiring inside. I had breached that spell by tossing a mercenary out of the window to break that illusion, and it would take something to circumvent her spell now. They had prepared for this attack and with Dimitri's expertise and assistance, they would overrun the death dealers in time.

Brigid could create an infallible illusion and sound barrier, but there was one connection she couldn't ward against. I moved deftly to the side, matching Kirnen's movements as he looked for an opportunity to stab me. Amidst the deadly dance that played out before me. I reached out for the connection in my mind, one forged out of love. It was different now, and it took a moment for me to illuminate the thread that had gone dark when I died. I had never tried to use this connection when I was under duress, but my daughter's voice whispered in my mind like a beacon in a windstorm.

Mom? Is that you?

Yes, baby. We are under attack. Call Rene on his cell. We need help.

I'm on it; just hold on.

Kirnen swung his spear toward my face and a fireball erupted in my palm and shot toward him. I stared in stunned silence as it penetrated his heart. The flames ignited his skin like papier mâché and spread outward like amber fingers as it consumed his flesh and vital organs. I staggered back as he fell to his knees.

CHAPTER 18

$\mathcal{T}$ime stilled as Kirnen clutched his disintegrating chest. A guttural scream escaped his dry lips as the flames devoured his skin. The once-powerful death dealer was wasting away before my eyes, consumed by the fire I had unleashed upon him.

The crackling sound of the flames saturated the air, mingling with his agonized screams. My eyes remained fixated on his crumbling corpse, with a mixture of dread and vindication twisting in my gut. The orange and yellow hues danced across his agonized face, casting an eerie shadow that seemed to reach toward me. A whispered reminder of my actions.

As the flames continued their relentless assault, his skin blackened and peeled away, before crumbling into gray ash. A shiver skated up my spine as I comprehended the weight of what I had done. I had harnessed my elemental power, this benign force, and unleashed it in a destructive manner on another being. The power I wielded was exhilarating and terrifying, but I couldn't shake the feeling of guilt that gnawed at my conscience.

When a final burst of fire exploded from Kirnen's chest, a plume of ash erupted where the vampire had knelt. The flames consumed him entirely, leaving only a swirling cloud of dust and the faint scent of burnt flesh in the air. The sight was both mesmerizing and horrifying as a squeak escaped from my lips.

As the last traces of smoke dissipated into the air and his ashes settled on the floor, I froze with a heavy breath. The weight of my actions shrouded me like a heavy cloak, a haunting reminder of the darkness I was capable of. Kirnen's disintegrating flesh had not only destroyed him physically, but ignited a turmoil within my own soul. I was the prophesied Blood Witch.

Guilt washed over me as I grappled with the choices I had made. I had taken a life, no matter how misdirected it might have been. The power I had tapped into had come with a cost that I was unsure I could pay, making me wonder if I could ever find redemption for what I had become.

In the wake of my remorse at Kirnen's death and the manner in which I allowed his demise, a dark shroud began to form close to me. I had seen Brigid's special ability several times, and I backed away, knowing she would step from her perfect hiding place any second. As her black robes emerged from the shroud, Dimitri stepped through the protection spell separating me from Cass and the rest of the clan.

His suit was perfect, and it was obvious Brigid had ensured nobody touched him, but his sneer was vicious as he approached me. "Kirnen was a fool. He declined Brigid's protection spell and now I must kill you myself. I prefer not to engage in such unpleasantness personally, but exceptions can be made for the king's whore."

I grunted. "You are just pissed because neither Cass nor I would have anything to do with you. Cassara was right. You are pathetic."

Dimitri hissed as he pulled a small dagger from his suit jacket. It didn't look that imposing, but if I knew Brigid at all, that blade was dipped in poison. Since I was cut off from Rene and his powerful blood, I trusted that the traitorous witch could kill me, given time.

My mind reached for the familiar thread in my mind. *Jana?*

I'm here, Mom.

My relief was palpable, but I kept my eyes trained on Dimitri. *Did you get a hold of Rene?*

I just got off the phone with him. He should be on his way to you now.

There was an explosion of wood at the door as Rene burst in and splinters erupted around the startled mercenaries. Their surprise was mirrored by the dark witch creating the barriers between me and the clan, but she flinched when Rene smashed against her barrier, and she was forced to drop all but the one separating us from Rene. She sucked in a breath when he smashed against it for the second time.

With her power focused on the growling overseer intent on my freedom, it left the mercenaries without any defense against the skilled death dealers. One by one, the black militia force fell by vampire hands until they were standing beside Rene, rushing the protection barrier.

Part of me wanted to unleash my power on Dimitri, to watch him burn as Kirnen had, but another part of me cried out in misery and pain. In the end, I was too weak to fight two assailants and Brigid was the more powerful of the two. I cursed under my breath as Dimitri used his preternatural speed to disappear through the open wall. A sliver of orange dusted the horizon as dawn threatened and I secretly hoped Dimitri smoldered in the sun before he found refuge.

Brigid was powerful, but she was also intelligent. With the mercenaries slain and Dimitri gone, she was alone. The shroud began to form around her, and I was well aware she would disappear in that effective glamor if it was allowed to escape her fully.

In that pivotal moment, as Brigid's fingers extended, weaving the threads of her powerful shroud, I knew only my power could halt it. The air seethed with anticipation, and a storm of magic swirled around me like a wind tunnel. With fierce determination, I focused on my own magic, the natural force that flowed through my veins and anchored my soul.

I stretched out my hand, trembling with the intensity of my building power, and directed my magic toward the thickening shroud. The air crackled with white energy as my power blasted into hers, bringing light to the darkness. I staggered under the strain and noticed she did as well, as the tug of war between our forces escalated. I desperately tried to unravel the threads of her shroud before it could envelop her and whisk her to safety.

As I poured my energy into the struggle, the protective barrier around us shimmered like a cocoon of light. It was weakening between her expenditure of power to form the shroud and the repeated attempts by Rene and the clan to breach its defenses. In the end, Brigid decided that she would rather fight me than Rene and the clan, and she reinforced that shield after the tendrils of the shroud began to dissipate.

Brigid's eyes blazed with fury as her shroud diminished under my relentless assault. Her lips moved with whispered incantations, as she called on a darkness that sent shivers down my spine. But I continued my assault, with my magic pushing against the tide of her malevolence. We both had protection barriers in place now, but she was fighting on two fronts.

With a final surge of energy, I focused on her black robes and used the last of my reserves. The dark witch's shroud shattered like broken glass, dissipating like mist in the morning sun. She staggered back, exposed and vulnerable, as her hold over her magic weakened, and Rene burst through her protection spell. I planned to channel my magic and knock her off balance, but Cass was far quicker than I.

Cass picked Brigid up by the throat and hissed at her with extended fangs. For a moment I thought she would bite the witch scratching her wrists and kicking her torso, but Cass simply twitched her wrist, and the resounding crack of Brigid's neck chilled my entire body as I slumped to the floor. Rene was at my side in seconds as Cass dropped Brigid's body unceremoniously to the floor.

My shoulders shook as I turned toward Rene, and the first tear escaped my eyes. Crimson tears flowed down my cheeks and stained his shirt. It wasn't Brigid I wept for. It was the betrayal and the fact she had forced Cass to kill her. She had manipulated so many people, including the coven high priestess and even with her death we would have to deal with the ramifications of her betrayal. We would still have to hunt down Dimitri and those who followed him, but without the powerful witch to aid him, it was only a matter of time before the death dealers and PSO officers caught up with him.

Cass knelt down and touched my shoulder. "You okay, honey? You had me worried there for a moment."

I sniffed before turning toward her. "I am sorry about Kirnen. He forced me to... kill him."

Cass grunted. "He was a traitor. He deserved what he got. I am only sorry you were forced to take care of that yourself. It was my job to protect you."

I shook my head. "You aren't a witch, Cass. You have no way to fight, one as powerful as Brigid. No vampire, with the exception of Rene, stands a chance against a senior witch."

The death dealers stood in silence, staring at me. It took me a moment to discern their looks of admiration. While my methods were different from theirs. I had proven far more powerful than the second-in-command of the coven. I had no idea if I could beat Ursula in a fight, and it was an experience I hoped to forgo. For now, the coven high priestess was avoiding a confrontation, and it was largely because the human delegate was furious with her. She was one small incident away from being disposed of, and she knew it.

Rene helped me to my feet, but my head spun as I stood. The ringing in my ears increased before I heard Rene shout my name and the room went dark.

CHAPTER 19

*U*nder the soft glow of the moon's subtle light, I stirred from the realm of dreams, with the warmth of silk sheets cradling me. They caressed my skin like a gentle touch from Rene's fingertips as I attempted to blink away the remnants of my slumber. The comforting smell of vanilla candles alerted me to my location, and I sighed as Rene's arms tightened around me. "I passed out, didn't I?"

Rene kissed my cheek. "You expended too much of your power. In time you will learn to harness mine through our connection so you may sustain yourself longer."

"I just want to stay here." In the intimate suite I now called home within the mansion, I realized I had sensed his presence before I even fully opened my eyes. Rene, my eternal partner in both life's challenges and its exquisite pleasures, was nestled beside me, his loving touch a reminder of his devotion. His fingers traced delicate patterns across my skin, as if choreographed by an ancient dance of desire. Every stroke ignited a firestorm of sensations that licked over my body, awakening my senses.

The air was infused with a subtle blend of scents, including Rene's lust. He had been waiting for me to wake, but hadn't wanted to interrupt my slumber. The soft rustle of fabric accompanied his restlessness, and a melody of affectionate intent filled the space between us. He tipped my chin up to meet his gaze. The reflection in his eyes would have stopped my heart had I still been human. Those unspoken words bound us together stronger than any spell. Love and commitment were our connection, and they would last an eternity.

As I closed the distance between us, my lips angling toward his, our eyes locked in a silent exchange. A language known only to two souls who would traverse the landscapes of undead life together. Time blurred as his lips connected to mine. The gentle collision sent a current of emotions coursing through me. Each kiss was a brushstroke on the canvas of our eternal bond, painting a portrait of love and commitment that would grow richer and more profound in the coming years.

Our bodies, attuned to one another's needs and desires, responded with a shared yearning that transcended our species or circumstances. Our love would deepen and mature, like a fine wine savored over time, and I looked forward to every pleasurable second.

As our embrace tightened and the space between our bodies narrowed, every hesitation or grain of uncertainty melted away. Our souls entwined in a symphony of heartbeats and hushed breaths as we made love slowly. The world outside faded into the background, and we allowed passion to replace duty and dedication.

I wasn't sure how long we remained confined to that bed, but I dozed in Rene's arms for some time with his caressing my shoulder before my curiosity got the better of me. "What happened in the training facility after I blacked out?"

"Constantine was outside when the mercenaries and clan members who helped Dimitri attempted to flee. They have all been sent to their eternal rest."

"I wondered where he was. I was so focused on Brigid and Dimitri, that I didn't really notice who else was in the room."

"Constantine takes loyalty quite seriously. He has requested that he be your personal adviser. It is... surprising that he would suspend his duties to the Shadow Phantom clan to undertake such a position."

I frowned. "But I want Cassara."

Rene kissed my cheek. "She is mine. If I renounce her, then she must regain her status over time."

"No. That isn't fair. So, if I take Constantine as an adviser, that means he lives with us?"

Rene grunted. "No. He would have his own suite, like Cassara does. Since we will be required to travel to the clans, he will travel with us. I will say that while Cassara strikes fear into many of the clans, she is still... young by vampire standards. Constantine is one of our oldest members and his skills are indisputably the best. Attacking you with Constantine as your adviser is... a death sentence."

"Cass would kill anyone who attacked me or you, anyway."

"True," Rene said.

My eyes narrowed. "This isn't just about me. He wants Cass to accept him."

Rene sighed. "It is true he has fancied Cassara since she began training, but Constantine is a patient man. He knew that not allowing her time to... experience life as a vampire would end any chance of a relationship."

"I thought some vampires chose human lovers and turned them so they could be together."

"That is true, but Cass is unique. She was never allowed to be herself in her human life. She has never truly been in love with a man."

"She likes the mortician," I said.

"She has many lovers, but she is not in love with any of them. The mortician is an intelligent man. He knows he could have a brief relationship with Cass, and it would be enjoyable, but there is no future in it."

"Do you think Cass is in love with Constantine? Is that why she avoids him?"

Rene sighed. "She fears becoming one of the women she helped in her human life. Some of those women loved their husbands but feared for their lives when they contacted Cass. Constantine would never hurt Cassara, but he is of the old world. He cannot stop his instinct to protect her."

"Oh dear. That is worse than asking her to wear a frilly dress."

Rene chuckled. "Yes, I suppose it is."

I was quiet for some time and my fingers traced a pattern on Rene's chest. "Will you tell me more about this king business? Constantine gave me the queen moniker because he anticipated your evolution."

Rene nodded. "I suspected that as well, but I don't know exactly how I will evolve."

"Do you feel any different? Now that we bonded, I mean?"

His fingers traced my shoulders. "Yes. I was becoming... anxious. But I can't say if that is because I was afraid you would reject me or the onset of the madness that afflicts my species as we age."

"But you don't feel that way now?"

"No. I am content. Happy."

I smiled at him. "Good. What do we do next?"

"I must introduce you to all the clans."

My body stilled. "There better not be any other wives."

He laughed. "No. You will be inducted into every clan. As the

FORTY DEATHS TILL US PART

only vampire with magic, the clan heads want you to have residency within the clans. Of course we have to formally introduce you, so there will be many vampire balls in your future."

I winced. "More parties?"

"Yes."

"Cass is going to hate me."

Rene chuckled. "She is used to it, and she can buy more dresses."

"Because she loves shopping so much," I teased.

"Yes, but Constantine will be forced to attend, and she will enjoy his disdain for such events."

"That is terrible of her... funny, though."

"I agree. Constantine is far too sure of himself. Cass is one of the few people to challenge him."

"You are one to talk. But I imagine that is one of the reasons Constantine loves her," I said.

Rene stared at me. "Thank you for choosing me."

I grunted. "I think that is the other way around. You are the most powerful man alive."

Rene shook his head. "There have been many overseers in our history. There is only one of you."

I licked my lips. "The prophecy didn't say much about me other than I am the Blood Witch."

He kissed my forehead. "You are my eternal bride. That is the only thing that matters. It is all you need to be."

I pressed closer to him. "I can do that."

His lips met mine in a gentle kiss that conveyed his immortal love. It wrapped around my soul like an unbreakable silver thread and the room blurred around us until he lifted his head.

I stared into his sparking eyes. "So, this is my magical, undead life?"

Find out what happens next in the Magical Midlife Death series by reading Forty is the New Dead.

Continue reading for a sample.

FORTY IS THE NEW DEAD
CHAPTER 1

I stood in the heart of the Shadow Demon mansion, nestled high in the mountains on the outskirts of Vancouver. The vast glass windows framed the ocean, a dark expanse under the night sky, with only a handful of boats still drifting. Most were safely docked at the distant marina, their lights twinkling faintly like fireflies in the summer dusk.

This was the second clan I had been inducted into since Shadow Bone, but I loved this location. There was something about the undercurrent of sound here, the relentless rhythm of waves crashing against the jagged rocks below; that spoke to me. It was a reminder of nature's unyielding power, a force that could not be tamed.

The living room was a blend of elegance and rustic charm, an open space that seemed to breathe within the surrounding forest. Polished wood floors gleamed under the soft glow of wrought-iron chandeliers, their design mimicking twisted branches. Plush, earth-toned sofas and chairs were arranged around a stone fireplace, its hearth bearing the marks of countless fires. The scent of burning cedar mingled with the salty sea air, creating a heady, comforting aroma.

Exposed wooden beams stretched across the ceiling, their rough-hewn surfaces telling tales of the ancient trees they once were. Shelves carved into the walls held a curated collection of artifacts and books, each piece telling a story of its own. The decor was a testament to the natural beauty outside; each item chosen with care, each placement a nod to the surrounding wilderness.

Cass moved to stand beside me. She held a wineglass in her hand and took a sip as she stared out at the water. "This place has the best view."

"It does. The people seemed nice too." I recalled my introduction to the Shadow Demon Clan, a moment strikingly similar to the one at Shadow Bone. Stepping out of mine and Rene's suite with Cass by my side, I felt the weight of countless eyes on me. The clan members lined the hallways and stairs, their gazes curious yet welcoming. Each face was a new chapter in this unfolding story, and I met them all, one by one, as I made my way toward Rene.

Rene was in the ballroom waiting for me. When I finally reached him, he embraced me and declared my acceptance into the clan. It was a powerful moment, one that marked the beginning of a new chapter in my life. Now, the introductions were over, and the clan was immersed in the festivities of my ball.

The ballroom area was alive with music, a band playing tunes that echoed through the grand hall. The joy and energy of the celebration were palpable, yet I couldn't shake the exhaustion from our plane ride last night and the limited sleep I'd managed to get. I had mingled with the guests, my smile genuine but my thoughts already drifting to the comfort of the morning, when I could finally turn in for some much-needed rest.

When Rene was in a deep conversation with the clan leader of Shadow Demon, I had left the ballroom to make my way to the living room overlooking the ocean. I wasn't surprised I had less than a minute alone before Cass joined me. Even within clan walls, she or Rene were never far from my side. Even with Brigid gone, one of them or Constantine was close to me.

Cass took another sip of her drink. "Yeah, this clan is pretty stable. We have few issues here. Rene chose the more... balanced clans to induct you into first."

I arched an eyebrow. "Balanced?"

"Ones that aren't as politically motivated."

Cass and I turned at the sound of footsteps behind us. A tall, attractive man with striking black hair and piercing blue eyes approached with a wineglass in his hand. His dark blue suit and white dress shirt, were paired with a bold red tie that immediately marked him as the leader of the Shadow Demon Clan.

I had met him briefly before Rene inducted me into the clan, and his presence now was both commanding and comforting. "Hello, Randal," I greeted, my voice steady despite the flutter of nerves in my stomach.

Randal smiled, a slow, knowing smile that seemed to hold a thousand secrets. "Welcome to the clan," he said, his voice smooth and warm, like the wine he held. He raised his glass slightly in a toast, his eyes never leaving mine. There was something about him that drew you in, made you feel seen and understood.

His gaze shifted briefly to Cass and then back to me. "I trust you're finding everything to your liking?"

"Very much so," I replied, returning his smile. "It's beautiful here."

Randal nodded, a look of satisfaction crossing his features. "I'm glad you like it. I'm hoping you will visit often and bring Cassara with you." He winked at me as he took another sip of his drink.

Cass rolled her eyes, but it was obvious Cass had yet another admirer. Though her quirky smile alerted me that she was fond of this one. "She may be a member of Shadow Demon, but I am not."

Randal shrugged casually. "You could be."

Cass grunted. "I go where Rene goes, Randal, and you know it."

Randal glanced at me. "He kept you with him because he is fond of you and needed a... confidant. He has Raven now and while he will always have affection for you, it is time for you to choose your own path. Even if it is not with my clan, I hope you will consider your own future. Not one Rene chose for you."

I wasn't sure I liked the turn in the conversation, but Cass glanced at me as if she was considering his words. "I know you mean well, Randal. But I chose to lead the death dealers after helping Rene create them, and they will always be my priority. No matter what clan they are from."

Randal nodded. "If that is your choice, then I respect it."

"Thank you," Cass said.

Randal turned to me. "Rene has changed a lot since your emergence. He is quite possessive of you. It looks good on him. I swear he almost smiled when he demonstrated your powers for us."

"I am trying to be transparent with the clans. I am learning to be a vampire, but most of my powers are new as well, and I can make mistakes."

Randal sighed. "Dimitri reported the incident that led to you impaling him in the foyer. I wish I had been around to see it. That vampire is a disgrace to us. I hope you keep an open mind with the other clans. Most believe you are a blessing. One that has given us a chance at saving our overseer. He brokered the peace treaty we all enjoy, and I am uncertain another could maintain it if he... lost interest in life."

Cass took a sip of her drink. "Rene won't lose interest in life. Not now."

Randal smiled at me. "I know. Our members won't consider you a witch, Raven. They will consider you an angel."

Cass grunted. "Don't bet on it, Randal."

Randal rolled his shoulders, bringing attention to his muscular form. "If they don't, they will find themselves with cement shoes at the bottom of the ocean."

Cass smiled before she winked at me. "You see why I like him."

Randal sighed. "If only you meant that as more than a friend."

Cass shook her head as if he was joking, but his gaze moved over her slim form, and I knew he wasn't.

The band in the other room finished their song and Randal motioned toward the door that led to the ballroom. "I must thank our entertainment for their performance this evening." He bowed to us and sauntered toward the ballroom.

"I like him," I said. Even the hard questions he asked were out of love for Cass. He honestly cared about her wellbeing regardless of which man she chose.

Cass stared out the window. "Me too. Just not in the way he wishes I did."

"May I ask why? He is gorgeous and seems genuine."

"He is. And he isn't a warrior, so he would never attempt to stand in my way if there was an altercation."

Part of me wondered if that was the problem. She wanted a partner. One that would fight by her side, just not one that would stand in front of her. Cass was just too good at what she did and the few men that matched her skill were all members of Shadow Phantom. And there was only one there that she had feelings for, despite her intention to ignore them.

"Cassara, there you are." A tall man who Cass had introduced as Leopold approached us.

"What can I do for you Leopold?" Cass asked with a deadpan voice.

"I just wanted to get to know Raven, since I am the frontrunner for the next election."

Cass huffed. "That is over fifty years away. It's a little early for voting."

Leopold shrugged. "Not really. We must adopt more progressive election techniques, similar to the humans."

Cass grunted. "I believe Dimitri said something similar to me."

Leopold smoothed his tie. "Dimitri was desperate to retain his power. I wish to be the next leader, not alter our traditions." He said he wanted to get to know me, but Leopold kept his eyes on Cassara and barely glanced my way.

"I hate politics," I said out loud before I could censor my remark.

Leopold glanced at me as if I were a bug. "It takes a certain intelligence to understand the intricacies of political power, it is not for the weak minded."

Cassara's eyes flickered with red. "I suggest you move along, Leopold. If I mention to Rene that you just inferred his woman has the mental acuity of a turnip, I'm sure he will take offense. Since he usually kills people who look at her wrong, I wouldn't worry about that election."

Leopold paled and glanced at me in fear. He bowed awkwardly before quickly moving toward the ballroom.

Cass sighed. "I wish Con were here."

I placed my glass on the windowsill. "Really?"

"Yeah, he would have killed that little prick and taken the punishment. It's kind of his thing. He knows Rene can't stay mad at him."

"Rene can't stay mad at you either," I said.

"Yeah, but I am his protector. Con is more of a hammer. Nobody expects him to play nice, even for Rene's sake."

"Honestly, I am surprised Con agreed to stay at Shadow Bone," I said.

Cass grunted. "He didn't. Rene gave him a direct order. It's rare for him to force Con's compliance and Con didn't take it well. I'm sure my death dealers will be exhausted when I return. Con will take his frustrations out in the ring if he doesn't have an opponent."

"I'm surprised he agreed then," I said.

"In the end, it comes down to Randal. Con knows he runs a tight ship and the security risk to you was minimal. Rene needed someone he trusts at Shadow Bone while we are gone."

"If Rene is the overseer, why would there be a threat in another clan?"

Cass was silent for a moment. "There have been reposts from every clam except Shadow Phantom that Dimitri is trying to subvert clan members to his cause."

"Has anyone betrayed us?"

"He has had a few takers. Usually vamps that have little standing in their clan or who are not well respected."

"I can't believe anyone would be so gullible. Dimitri is a snake."

"Yeah, but after what happened with his brother, we are not taking any chances with your security."

A young vamp strolled by, and his eyes moved over Cassara. "You look ravishing, Miss James."

Cass nodded. "Thanks Franklin."

I had to agree with the young blond vampire. Cassara's black ruffled dress was stunning. The layers of tulle whispered over the floor as she walked while the tight bodice accented her waist. My dress was silky and fitted. It wasn't something I would normally have chosen, especially in white, but Rene had bought it for me and the material was like butterfly wings on my skin.

He smiled at me. "You look beautiful as well, Raven.

Welcome to the clan. I hope you will have the chance to visit often. We do night cruises regularly on our private yacht."

"That sounds amazing. I would love to..."

Rene's hand slipped around my waist, and I jumped. "Damn it Rene. You keep this up and I am going to invest in that bell."

"Sorry, Raven. We must go." He nodded politely to Franklin before escorting me toward the stairwell that led to the private rooms.

Cass said nothing as she followed us upstairs, but closed the door behind us when we entered our private suite. "What is going on?"

The suite at Shadow Demon had a similar layout to the one at Shadow Bone, with a connecting suite for Cass, but the decor was more modern with pine furniture.

Rene pointed to her door. "Get changed. We must leave immediately. There has been an attack."

Cass went to her suite as Rene and I changed from our formal wear. Cass was back in a few minutes wearing her leather one piece. She still had her makeup on, but she had slicked her hair back and the effect made her appear even more deadly.

I had changed into a pair of black pants and a white blouse before grabbing a red leather jacket from the closet. Rene had explained I didn't need to pack clothes, as every clan had a suite with a full wardrobe waiting for us.

We were downstairs and getting into the limousine before most of the clan realized we had left the party.

We were pulling away from the mansion before Cass spoke. "Is it another attack from Dimitri's people? He is getting more brazen. He must have subverted some additional members from either Shadow Bone or another clan."

Rene shook his head. "This was not Dimitri, and Constantine has confirmed that no further members of Shadow Bone have defected."

"It wasn't a vampire attack?" Cass asked.

"Several humans were attacked and killed, but the perpetrators were not vampire."

Cass frowned. "Why would we concern ourselves with human perpetrators?"

Rene pulled out his phone and pulled up a picture. He showed it to Cass and me. The man's head was barely attached to his body. There was so much blood on his clothes, I had no idea what color his jacket had been. The wounds on his torso were just as savage and he looked like he had been through a shredder.

She stared at the image. "An animal attack?"

"Constantine was called to investigate this by William as the humans were ripped apart in a back alley of a pub. He has confirmed that the killer is a lycan. He can smell it on the bodies."

Cassara's eyes widened. "That is impossible. They have been extinct for a thousand years."

Rene put his phone away and leaned back in his seat. "Nobody is more surprised by this development than me. I was sure they were extinct. I hunted the last of the local pack myself with Constantine and members of Shadow Phantom."

My emotions churned in a turbulent mix of regret and wonder. Part of me was mortified by the image of blood and violence Rene had showed us. The gore and devastation were hard to shake. Yet, there was another part of me, a quieter voice, that felt a pang of sorrow for the exterminated lycans.

It was difficult to reconcile these feelings. The vampires had taught me that no species could be entirely bad. I had seen their complexities, their struggles, and their capacity for both cruelty and compassion. It was a lesson I couldn't ignore, one that made me question the sweeping generalizations about the lycans. Surely, when their species was thriving, there had been some good people among them, individuals who didn't fit the monstrous mold we so often attributed to them.

But this was not a sentiment I could share with Rene. His experiences, his convictions, were deeply rooted in a different reality. Voicing my doubts would be like challenging the very foundation of his beliefs, something I wasn't ready to do. Instead, I kept my thoughts to myself, silently wrestling with the conflicting emotions.

"Where do you think they have been hiding and what brought them out now?" Cass asked.

Rene sighed. "I assume they hid when I killed the clan heads. With the king gone, they had no way of fighting me. I thought we had tracked down the stragglers in the pack."

My voice was barely a whisper. "What will you do if they are back?"

"They cannot be allowed to kill the humans. William lacks the technology to fight them. Their weapons are designed to kill vampires and will have little effect on a lycan. Their human guns are better, but they must hit the lycan dozens of times to slow it down and a werewolf is much faster and stronger than a human. They must be put down before they start turning the mundanes."

I let out a slow breath. "So you plan to exterminate them? Again."

FORTY IS THE NEW DEAD
CHAPTER 2

The limo rolled to a stop in the private section of the airport, and Rene stepped out with his usual grace. He extended his hand toward me, his eyes steady and reassuring. I took it, allowing him to guide me from the back seat, my boot heels clicking softly on the pavement. Ahead of us, a large private jet waited just outside the hangar, its sleek lines and powerful presence glinting against the exterior lighting.

As we ascended the stairs to board, I couldn't help but appreciate the aircraft. It was immaculate, the kind of plane that whispered of wealth and exclusivity. The interior boasted cream leather seats, polished wood accents, and soft lighting that created an atmosphere of opulence and comfort. Rene led me to our seats, and I sank into the sumptuous cushion, the material cool and smooth against my skin.

Despite the luxury surrounding me, my mind was a whirl of mixed emotions. Rene hadn't answered my question. I glanced at him, his face a picture of calm as he settled in beside me. What was he thinking? What was he hiding? The silence between us was thick, heavy with unspoken words as Cass took a seat opposite us.

I tried to focus on the present, the gentle hum of the jet's engines as it prepared for takeoff, the subtle scent of leather and expensive cologne filling the cabin. But my thoughts kept drifting back to our conversation about the lycans. I wanted answers, clarity, but I was surrounded by luxury and uncertainty.

The ride was relatively quick and none of us spoke. If this was a lycan attack, Cass was unprepared for the first time in hundreds of years. Once we landed and the private jet rolled to a stop, Rene was out of his seat moving toward the exit. We were off the plane and getting into the waiting limo in seconds.

Rene's phone chimed as we pulled out of the airport. His face hardened as he read the text.

"What is it?" I asked.

"Constantine found another body in an adjacent alley. The bite marks are smaller on the second man. There is more than one rogue lycan."

Cass stared at Rene. "How far away is the attack site?"

Rene had told us it happened in an alley outside a pub in Black Blossom, but he hadn't supplied the address or name of the establishment.

"We are only ten minutes away. Constantine has called William, and the PSO is on site. The area is locked down. We don't need the public to panic until we understand what is going on."

I sighed. "Is there anyway someone could fake this attack? Dimitri would love to cause dissension between the witches, humans, and vampires. The return of the lycans could have that effect."

Cass narrowed her eyes on me. "The wounds would be easy enough to fake, but how would you fake a lycan's scent?"

Rene shook his head. "Very few vampires would be able to detect the difference between a wolf and a lycan. The smell is similar, but lycans are more... acrid. But Constantine knows that scent well. I do not believe he could be fooled that easily."

"He hasn't smelled a lycan in a thousand years. He was young when you exterminated the last of the lycan pack... or thought you did."

Rene glanced out the window as we cruised through the downtown streets. "Due to advancements in modern technology, I suppose it is possible. We need a physical description of the attacker, or better yet, a body. We must find this aggressor, no matter what species it belongs to."

The limo tuned onto a side street and passed several men in black PSO tactical gear.

The vehicle rolled to a stop in a narrow alley; the tires crunching over broken glass and debris. Beside a rusty blue garbage bin, Constantine stood like a grim silhouette in the dim light. He was motionless, except for his eyes, which tracked our approach with a steady intensity. At his feet lay a body, covered with a white sheet that was rapidly turning crimson as blood soaked through it.

We exited the limo with the night air heavy with the scent of decay and iron. My steps were slow and deliberate, each one bringing me closer to the grim reality before us. As we neared, Constantine knelt down, his movements precise and respectful. With a careful grip, he pulled back the sheet, revealing the damage underneath.

The sight was worse than the photos had suggested. Jagged wounds marred the man's flesh, cruel and haphazard, as if inflicted in a frenzy. The blood was a stark, visceral reminder of the violence that had occurred. My stomach churned, but I forced myself to remain composed.

Rene inhaled deeply beside me, and both Cass and I turned to him instinctively. His face was a mask of control, but his eyes spoke volumes. They held a mix of fury and sorrow, a deep well of emotions that he rarely let surface. I could see him processing the scene, the implications of such brutality.

"Constantine is correct. This was a lycan kill," he said.

Con pointed down the alley. "The other body is down there and to the right. One alley over."

Rene's gaze didn't waver from the body. "This wasn't just an attack," he said, his tone measured but laced with an undercurrent of anger. "It was a message."

"What kind of message is this?" I asked in a low tone.

"One to declare war," Rene growled.

Con motioned Cass to his side as he led us down the alley. "Were there any issues at Shadow Demon?"

Cass shook her head. "Just a rude vampire. Leopold implied that the salt had fallen off Raven's cracker. Other than that, it was all speeches, dancing, and schmoozing. Basically, your favorite things in life."

Con grunted. "Perhaps I was better off here. I am the only one besides Rene who would have recognized this as a lycan kill."

Cass frowned as we walked toward the second alleyway. "Maybe they were counting on that."

"What makes you say that?"

Cass shook her head. "Just a feeling, I guess. Had you not been on scene, a vicious animal attack would have been reported to Rene and he would not have returned so soon."

Con was quiet as we walked. "That would suggest that someone's feeding the lycans information. Only the clan, Ursula, and William, knew that Rene was leaving to induct Raven to the Shadow Demon clan."

"Yeah, that's what scares me," Cass said as we approached a second body covered in a sheet. A PSO officer nodded to Constantine and moved away as Con knelt down and pulled back the covering.

The young man, who looked like he was in his early twenties, had blond hair, but it was plastered to his face with blood. His wounds were similar to his friend in the other alley, but the bite marks were noticeably smaller.

Rebe sighed. "This one is likely a female. They are much smaller in lycan form."

"You are going to kill a woman?" I said as goosebumps formed over my skin. I was impervious to the cold, but my body still reacted to emotional trauma.

Rene tuned to me. "If the rogue were a female vamp, would you have me leave her on the street to kill the innocent?"

I closed my eyes and took a breath. "No, of course not. But how do we know if these lycans were turned by their choice? If you unleash a fledgling on the populace, it would likely attack because it can't control its urges. Would lycans be the same?"

Rene returned his gaze to the dead bodies. "It is the same for lycans. Possibly worse. Their transition rates are lower than ours and they never existed at a time where they could test for compatibility."

"If they were alive today, is that something that would work for them?"

"I honestly don't know. It took decades to perfect the technology that allows us to test human blood for viability. Theoretically, it is possible the lycans could have done the same had their king not driven them to war."

Cass knelt down and placed her hand around the dead man's wrist and lifted it to expose his smart watch. There was a small red light flashing on the watch. She removed the watch and stood before pulling out her phone and hitting a contact.

"Hello, Cass."

"Julian, I am at the scene of an attack. The victim has a smart watch. I think there may be a video feed. Can you access it?"

"Read me the serial number on the back and give me the

victim's phone number. I will see if that model had that capability."

Cass read him the serial number of the watch as she searched the body for a phone. She found it in the young man's pocket and held it to his face to unlock it before reading the number off to Julian.

I could hear Julian typing on the other end of the line. "You are right, this model has a live feed. Give me some time to hack the server. I will send you the info once I have it."

Cass disconnected her call and turned to the PSO officer who stood a few feet away. "Hey, can you tell me what you have learned about the victims?"

The PSO officer approached her. "We interviewed the people at the pub. The two men were playing darts and having a few beers. They were not overly intoxicated when they left but over the legal limit to drive."

"Do you have any ideas why they were targeted?"

He shook his head. "We believe it was a crime of opportunity. They are college students, but many of the clientele at the pub are. This is a mundane bar. Few witches come here, and I have never seen a vamp present."

"You come here yourself?" Cass asked.

"My brother is in college. I have met him and his friends here a few times. I want this asshole found." He glanced at Rene. "Whatever did this is going down. The PSO has one policy for rogues, regardless of species."

Rene nodded. "I agree with William's policies in this regard."

Cassara's phone beeped, and she played a video that Julian had sent her. She sucked in a breath as her eyes flickered. "It's not a prank. They are lycan."

"Show me," Rene demanded.

Cass held out her phone to Rene and me, her face pale with tension. On the screen, a video played from the angle of a watch, moving erratically with the man's wrist as he walked. There was no sound, just the silent, grainy footage that told a story more terrifying than words ever could.

A shadow flickered in the alley, almost imperceptible at first. Then, in a sudden, horrifying burst of motion, a monster attacked the man's friend. The watch caught the scene in fragments; the camera shaking wildly. The half-man, half-beast creature came into view, its long claws gleaming in the dim light, its wolf-like head snarling with savage fury. It slashed at the victim's chest, the brutality of the attack clear even without sound.

The young man bolted, the view from the watch shifting wildly as he ran. He dashed down an adjacent lane. I could imagine his ragged breath and the scent of his fear. But I already knew how this ended. A smaller werewolf appeared, stepping in front of him with predatory grace. Its claws flashed, slashing him viciously. He staggered and tried to keep moving, but the wounds were too severe.

Eventually, he went down, the watch camera capturing the final moments of his desperate fight. The lens aimed at a streetlight down the lane, the bright, cold glow a stark contrast to the darkness and violence that had just unfolded. The video ended abruptly, leaving a heavy silence in its wake.

I looked up at Rene, my heart pounding. His face was set in stone, his eyes a storm of controlled rage. Cass' hand trembled slightly as she lowered her phone. The reality of the horror we had just witnessed sinking in.

"This was no random attack," Rene said quietly, his voice barely above a whisper. "This was calculated. Deliberate. The victims were not the true target. This was a warning."

"Of what?" Cass asked.

Constantine's tone was so low it whispered in the wind. "Of what is to come."

Rene tuned to Constantine. "Alert all the clan heads

immediately. Revive lycan protocols. All death dealers and warriors who are less than a thousand years old must be trained. There are few alive who are experienced at fighting them."

Cass shook her head. "I can't believe I am like a fledgling again," she said.

Con glanced down at her. "This is not like fighting a vampire, witch, or human. Lycan blood and venom is lethal to us. Only Rene has been successful in purging its toxins from his system. Every other vampire exposed to it died."

Cass pursed her lips. "I know the stories. But that is a two-way street. Our venom is lethal to them, too."

"Yes. But if you get close enough to bite one, then you are dead. The lycans had the same philosophy we did when it came to war. If you are going down, take your enemy with you. They will bite you, and both you and your attacker will die. I have buried many vampires with their murderers and do not wish to do it again. Especially with you."

Cass turned to me. "You will be training with me and my death dealers tomorrow."

Rene took a step toward her. "No Cassara. You have never fought a lycan and were never trained in the tactics needed to survive. You cannot teach what you do not know. Constantine will take interim leadership of the death dealers at Shadow Bone. He will assign a Shadow Phantom warrior with the appropriate skills to each clan to do the same. He will mentor you and your team until this threat is neutralized."

Cass looked like Rene had slapped her. I wasn't sure if it was the demotion or the impression that Rene didn't trust her to lead, but she nodded curtly and lowered her head. "You have command Constantine." Her words were cold, but I knew she wouldn't disobey a direct order.

Rene's hands fisted at his sides. He was not required to explain himself as overseer, but this was not just any order. "Cass, you have to understand. I would cut off my right arm rather than lose you. This is not a decision I take lightly. Shadow Phantom is the only clan with the resources and the experience to combat this threat. I have no doubt you will pick up the skills needed to lead your team."

Cass met his gaze, but there was still some doubt there. "I understand."

Rene stared at her. "I expect you to make things difficult for Constantine. He has had little in the way of a challenge. Do not go easy on him."

Cassara's lip twitched. "As if I ever would."

Constantine tightened the strap on his vest. The large sword on his back was a new addition to his gear, and I hadn't had a chance to ask why he chose a broadsword. "There are twenty members of my clan that have some experience with lycans. Since lycans only live to about six hundred under the best of circumstances, it stands to reason that they have no pack members with the skills needed to fight us."

Rene snorted. "Do not be so sure. We have had many members go missing over the centuries. We attributed it to human separatists or dark witches. It may have been the lycans all along."

I was still reeling at Constantine's last comment. I didn't know anything about the lycans. Not really. "They aren't immortal?"

Rene shook his head. "No. They have a lower turning ratio than we do, but they have the ability to bear children. Their mating habits ensured births were low and only happened with a chosen mate, but it kept our numbers fairly even before the war."

"What do we do next?" I asked.

Rene motioned to the PSO officer. "Take us to the pub. I want to confirm this was a target of opportunity and see if we can discern why they chose this location. They did not try to turn these humans, they were killed for sport."

The PSO officer nodded, and we began to follow him back toward the pub when Rene's phone went off.

He growled as he read the text. "We must leave. Shadow Bone has been attacked."

Find out what happens next in the Magical Midlife Death series by reading Forty is the New Dead.

ALSO BY TIA DIDMON

TIA HAS WRITTEN OVER 70 BOOKS. FOR A COMPLETE LIST AND A READING ORDER VISIT:

HTTPS://TIADIDMON.COM/BOOK-LIST/

ABOUT THE AUTHOR

Tia Didmon is a USA Today bestselling author of paranormal women's fiction and provocative paranormal romance. When Tia isn't busy writing about sexy shifters and dreamy demons, she spends her time binge-watching The Order and reruns of The Vampire Diaries, cooking with her daughter, and serving her cat. Her love of writing stems from a self-diagnosed book addiction.

Subscribe to Tia's newsletter at tiadidmon.com for a free book and start your journey through Tia's supernatural world today!

CONNECT WITH ME!

I love interacting with my readers. Follow me on your favorite platforms and/or message me through my website or Facebook.

Website - https://tiadidmon.com
Email – books@tiadidmon.com
Booksprout - https://booksprout.co/author/4408/tia-didmon

f facebook.com/tiadidmonauthor
X x.com/TiaDidmon
O instagram.com/tiadidmon
BB bookbub.com/authors/tia-didmon
a amazon.com/author/tiadidmon
g goodreads.com/tiadidmon